KILLER WITHIN

ALSO BY S. E. GREEN

Killer Instinct

KILLERWITHIN

S. E. GREEN

SIMON PULSE NEW YORK LONDON TORONTO SYDNEY NEW DELHI

SIMON PULSE

An imprint of Simon & Schuster Children's Publishing Division

1230 Avenue of the Americas, New York, NY 10020

First Simon Pulse hardcover edition May 2015

Text copyright © 2015 by Shannon Greenland

Jacket photograph copyright © 2015 by Getty Images

For information about special discounts for bulk purchases,

please contact Simon & Schuster Special Sales at 1-866-506-1949

or business@simonandschuster.com.

The Simon & Schuster Speakers Bureau can bring authors

to your live event. For more information or to book an event contact the

Simon & Schuster Speakers Bureau at 1-866-248-3049

or visit our website at www.simonspeakers.com.

Jacket designed by Jessica Handelman

Interior designed by Mike Rosamilia

The text of this book was set in Minion Pro.

Manufactured in the United States of America

2 4 6 8 10 9 7 5 3 1

Library of Congress Cataloging-in-Publication Data

Green, S. E., 1971–

Killer within / S. E. Green. — First Simon Pulse hardcover edition.

p. cm.

"A Killer Instinct Novel."

Summary: Disturbed Lane resumes her role as the Masked Savior, but an admirer becomes a copycat, assaulting the defenseless. And Lane also suspects someone is spying on her. Someone who knows her secrets.

[1. Criminals—Fiction. 2. Heroes—Fiction. 3. Family life—Washington (D.C.)—Fiction. 4. Interpersonal relations—Fiction. 5. Criminal investigation—Fiction. 6. Washington (D.C.)—Fiction.] I. Title.

PZ7.G82632Kiq 2015   [Fic]—dc23   2014022802

ISBN 978-1-4814-0288-0 (hc)

ISBN 978-1-4814-0290-3 (eBook)

Chapter One

I DUCK IN THE SHADOWS BESIDE THE DUMPSTER and wait. Beneath my mask I tune every sense to the night surrounding me.

Down the alley two cats scuffle.

Four stories up a woman and a man argue.

All around me snowflakes fall and wet the cement.

A rat sidles out from beneath the Dumpster, and I immediately move. I don't do rats.

I race to the end of the alley and spin around. My gaze flicks from shadow to shadow, but I don't see movement.

Maybe it's all in my head—this person I think is following me.

It's been three months since I killed the Decapitator.

It's been three months of nightly outings. Looking. Waiting.

Hunting. Trying to satisfy the urges that don't seem to be satiable. Even *I* know I'm wasting my talents.

Talents . . .

With my position in the FBI and your innate talents . . . We'll be great. We'll go down in history as the most infamous serial killers never caught.

I shake my mom's annoying voice from my head. I just want her to stay the hell out of my thoughts. But she won't. She pops in constantly. Frustratingly so. I wish I could reach inside my head, grab that section of my brain, and yank it out.

But I do what I always do. Bury it and refocus.

Four weeks ago I caught the freshman who graffitied the football field. I tied him up and left him on the fifty-yard line for the coaches to find.

Three weeks ago I shaved the captain of the cheerleaders' head. She'd "jokingly" done the same to a freshman girl who had passed out at a party.

Two weeks ago I caught a twelve-year-old girl stealing a Snickers bar from the 7-Eleven down the street. I made her go and confess.

And last week I kicked this kid's ass for swatting his dog with a rolled-up magazine. I do *not* put up with animal abusers. They rank pretty high on my hit list.

Yet all these things are beneath me. They're juvenile. But I just don't know what else to do. I need to feel alive again. I need adrenaline surging through my veins. But the last time I did was three months ago in the kill room with Zach and the Decapitator.

Down the alley a door opens, and I flatten myself along the wet brick wall. This is it. This is what I've been waiting for. Tonight will make up for the past frustrating months.

John Jacks Jones. His parents had a strange sense of humor when they named him. Age twenty-one. Caucasian. Drug dealer. I was first introduced to him and his partner, Aisha Olive, in Judge Penn's court—where I like to spend my spare time. John Jacks Jones, or Jacks as everyone calls him, is the worst kind of drug dealer. He and Aisha target the kids.

One week ago an eleven-year-old overdosed on pills, and Aisha and Jacks landed in Penn's court. They were released for lack of evidence, and that's when I first started trailing them. In the last five days I've witnessed them selling to three different kids. Yes, Jacks is definitely worthy of my focus. As is Aisha.

He coughs and spits, then lights up a cigarette. His phone rings and he answers it. "Yeah?"

As he listens, I take my Taser from my cargo pocket. Slowly I make my way down the alley and through the snow toward him. I size him up. Five foot ten. One hundred seventy-five pounds. Dark hair and goatee. Jeans. Jacket. Looks ordinary enough. I know from the past week of following him that he carries a gun.

"And what'd he say?" Pause. "Fuck him, man. If I say it's a grand, then it's a grand."

Ever since my mom dropped the f-bomb in the kill room, I've decided I don't care for the word.

As he listens to whoever's on the other end, I close the last few feet between us.

I lift my Taser . . . and pause.

My finger hovers over the trigger as I stare at the back of his head.

Pull the trigger!

"All right, later tonight, then." Jacks clicks off, flicks his cigarette into the snow, and walks back through the door he came out of.

I stand for a moment, finger still hovering over the trigger, staring at the closed door.

What the hell? Months ago I would've already had him tasered, zip-tied, and ready for whatever I had in store for him. I'm way off my game. And I have no clue why.

I turn the Taser around and study the barbs. *Shoot yourself, Lane. Maybe that'll bring you back to life.*

I get home a little before my midnight curfew to find Daisy in my bed. I take a breath and swallow it so I don't give in to the overwhelming urge to bitch at her.

My sister yawns. "Hey, where have you been?"

I give my standard lie. "The coffee shop."

She sits up. "I didn't see you there."

"I'm sorry?"

"I went to keep you company. Tried calling you too."

This isn't good. "New coffee shop. And I turn my phone off for *quiet* time."

I hope she gets my emphasis.

"Oh."

Apparently she does. Retreating to my walk-in closet, I quickly change into my sleep shirt. It's been like this since our mom died. Me and Daisy. Two peas. She's driving me nuts.

Her sudden connection to me wouldn't be such a shock if it weren't the complete opposite of the way things used to be. I find myself wishing more than I should that she'd go back to hating and ignoring me.

At least I'd get some me time.

"I'll go with you sometime if you want the company."

From inside my closet I close my eyes. I've got to figure this out. Me. Her. *Me.*

I flick the closet light off and shuffle back into my room. "Sleeping here tonight?" I ask, already knowing the answer.

She blinks her blue eyes. "If that's okay?"

I pull the covers back and climb in. "Sure."

As usual, she's asleep in five minutes and I lie awake for an hour. I never used to have problems sleeping. But over the past few months it seems me and sleep aren't getting along too well.

Daisy's breathing deepens. I focus on its cadence, thinking of her and Justin. I'm so happy neither of them inherited our mother's darkness. And that thought causes my mind to drift—as it has been doing lately—to years past and buried memories. . . .

Mom gives me several Barbie dolls. "If you feel anything, I want you to take it out on them, okay?"

I nod my eight-year-old head.

Days later she steps into my room, and I hand her a box full of Barbie body parts that I ripped and chewed off.

She soothes her hand over my braided hair. "Good girl. I'll get you more."

I am who I am, and she'd been grooming me from the start. I just never realized it until after her death.

Before. After. I've been thinking in those two terms a lot. How I was before she died—focused, together. And how I am after—scattered, lost.

Before. After.

After I killed her. The Decapitator. My mother.

Chapter Two

THE NEXT MORNING MY FIRST-PERIOD TA job rolls around, and I go straight to Mr. Bealles, our librarian.

He glances up from the circulation desk. "Hey, Slim."

It's always odd to me when teachers call me by my nickname. "Anything for me to do?"

He nods his bald head to the left. "Just shelve those books."

Quickly I do and then head straight to my usual computer station. As I'm logging on, my best friend, Reggie, texts me. CAN U TALK?

I dial her number. "What's up?"

"You doing okay today?"

No, but of course I don't say this. "Yeah, Reg. All good."

"Mm-hmm."

She knows I'm lying.

"All right," she says, "but the last few times we've talked you've been even more *short and sweet* than usual."

Because everyone's in my business, and I'm about to erupt if I don't figure out my shit. "Listen, I've got to go."

"Lane . . . I miss your mom too. You barely talk about her. I worry that you're not dealing with things."

"I'm dealing," I reassure her.

She sighs. "Well, I'm barely dealing. And I wasn't even her daughter."

I pause. Sometimes I forget how close Reggie and my mom were.

"Just know . . . know that you can *talk to me*," she emphasizes. "About anything. Okay?"

My heart softens. Reggie really is a good friend. But what am I supposed to say? That I decapitated my mother like she had done to so many others? That the loving woman Reggie mourns was a monster?

"Okay, Reg," I say instead. "Thanks for being you."

I feel her smile through the phone. "Love you, girl. I'll bug you later."

This makes me chuckle. Just a little.

"I'm sorry. Was that a *laugh* I just heard?"

"Bye, Reg." I click off and spend the next ten minutes

researching Jacks and Aisha, although I don't discover anything new.

"Hey, you."

I glance up. *Zach.* My ex-boyfriend. Sort of. Our relationship is so much more complicated than that. We've done a good job of politely acknowledging each other over the past months. It's not like we can avoid the other, going to the same school and all. But actually exchanging words? This is a first.

And just the sight of him standing in all his tall, lean, dark-haired cuteness makes me genuinely smile. "Hey."

The terrifying image of him in my mother's kill room flashes across my brain, and I shove it away. I can't think about that. I won't.

His brows twitch like he just picked up on my thoughts, and I purposefully glance over to the bookshelf where he gave me my first orgasm. He glances too, and I wonder if he's remembering as well.

Zach brings his dark eyes back to mine. "Wanted to let you know Daisy called me last night."

"What? Why?"

"Worried about you. Wanted to know if I'd seen you."

I sigh. "Sorry about that."

He props his hip on the desk, and I become hyperaware of his warmth and his boy-scented body wash. His eyes roam over me in that way they do when he takes in my red curly hair, green eyes, and pale freckly face.

"Her mom died. Be patient."

My mom died too. Why don't people seem to remember this? This is what I want to say but instead reply, "Well, thanks for letting me know."

He gives me a gentle, seemingly sad smile, and I want to ask him if he's doing okay but don't. I'm not sure why. Maybe because then he'll ask about me, and I really can't handle his probing. Or maybe because deep down I suspect he's not doing well, and I don't want to add that guilt to everything else going on in my brain.

A few quiet seconds tick by, and he gives me a nod before heading off.

If I could change schools, I would. I'm sick of the looks, the gossip, the hushed tones. This whole thing should've blown over by now, but it hasn't.

I'm Lane, niece to the Decapitator and daughter to the FBI director who lost her life saving my friend Zach. Or at least that's what everyone believes.

I am my mother's daughter. I am a killer.

That's what I really am, and the reminder has something twitching inside me. I need to figure things out. *Soon.* Or that twitch is going to spiral violently out of control.

Yet I had my chance last night with Jacks and didn't take it.

It's been three—long—months since I've experienced that kick in my heart, that swell in my veins. Three months since I killed my mother.

Though I'm not completely ready to admit it, in a crevice of my brain the thought sits there. Circling. Warming. A *kill* is what I need to get myself back on track. But with a premeditated kill I will cross the line I've been teetering on. Once I step over that line, it can't be undone.

Chapter Three

THAT NIGHT VICTOR, MY STEPDAD, MAKES lasagna for dinner. After Mom's death he's gone way above in the parent department. He's home by six, and family dinner is every night at seven.

Dinner we're *all* expected to be at. Dinner everyone seems to need but me.

"Dr. Depof suggested I make a new friend," Justin, my younger brother, is saying. "And so I said hi to Christopher today and I've never done that before."

"How did that make you feel?" Victor parrots Dr. Depof, our family grief counselor.

"It made me feel really good about myself."

It makes me feel like I want to stab myself in the eye.

Victor turns to Daisy. "How'd you do on your history exam?"

She brightens. "A lot better than I thought."

"Good, Daisy!" he verbally applauds.

They all smile at each other, and I swallow the overwhelming desire to scream.

Now is the point in dinner where everyone gets contemplative and silent as they eat lasagna and pretend they're *healing*.

Ugh.

But first Victor turns to me, the rock. "Lane, all good today? Anything to report?"

"Fine," I reply as he expects.

"You going out again tonight?" he asks.

"Yes." I'm going after Jacks again. And this time I *will* get him.

"Maybe you should try staying in. . . ."

I look him in the eyes, and way in their depths I catch a glimpse of the stepdad he used to be before all this went down. Strong. Kind. Loving. Solid. Does this whole *healing* thing wear him out as much as it does me? Is he tired of being selfless, forcing optimism, and hiding his real grief for our sake?

"Okay," I reluctantly agree. "I'll stay in."

I swear I hear a sigh of relief. That, coupled with Daisy's and Justin's dual smiles, gives me a pang of guilt for being gone so much.

I volunteer to do dishes, as I often do. I have a theory that the more steadfast I am around the house—the more chores I do—the more freedom I receive. So far it's a theory that works.

Victor goes into what used to be my mom's office, and my brother and sister disappear upstairs. I turn on the news and run a sink of soapy water.

"The Masked Savior has gone too far," a reporter is saying.

I perk up. The Masked Savior is what the news stupidly dubbed me back when I completed my first vigilante act—the Weasel, the rapist.

They flash a website up on the screen. I look at the Masked Savior URL. What the hell? I have my own site?

"Alleged drug dealer John Jacks Jones was found beaten to near death in an alley off MLK. He was—"

Wait a minute. *What?*

That's the same alley I'd been in last night when I swore someone was following me. But he was fine when I left, when I couldn't go through with things.

The reporter goes on to describe the messy bludgeoning details. Tasered first. Zip-tied. Beaten with a baseball bat. Left in the alley. Found by some homeless guy.

I would never have done it that way.

"Witnesses said they saw a person dressed in all black and wearing a mask. . . ." The reporter goes on to detail how Jacks was allegedly a member of a local gang.

Allege. Alleged. Allegedly. I hate all forms of that word. That's a cover-your-ass word. They flash a picture of Jacks on to the screen, and I think of last night and how I froze up.

The reporter transitions to another story, and I dry my hands and go get my laptop. I bring up my very own URL and holy damn, sure enough, the Masked Savior has a site.

And apparently quite a following. Not only are there details on the acts I actually did before Mom—the rapist, the drunk driver, the animal abuser, the human trafficker—but there are several more I'm getting credit for that I didn't do. Like Jacks.

This isn't good. This *so* isn't good.

I click into the forum and read some of the posts.

[j_d_l] The M. Savior should've overdosed JJJ like he did those kids.

[KellyKat] What's up with shaving that girl's head?

[HellsBells] Hey, homies, I'm new. What up?

I continue reading through the multitude of comments as everyone discusses the various vigilante acts. People like what I'm doing enough to have dedicated a whole site to me. While that makes me feel honored and justified, it also concerns me. I don't want or need a fan club. I can't afford to have people doing stuff "in my name."

Anonymity is essential. It's what I need. What I want. The time and space to be me.

The time and space to be me . . .

My gaze trails back to the comment about Jacks. I need to figure out who did this to him—who impersonated me, *copy-catted* me, and beat him to near death. He has a partner, Aisha. Was *she* the one I felt watching? Did something go wrong between them and did they have a fight?

I plug my flash drive in and bring up Aisha's picture and the information I already have on her. When I first saw her in Penn's court, she was very pretty with her dark ponytail and perfect makeup. I remember thinking how she looked more like a model than a drug dealer.

Then again, I don't look like who I am either.

I zoom in on her picture and her dark brown eyes, and I study them. Sure she's smiling, but there's something just not there. The smile is on her lips, but definitely not in her eyes. Those eyes . . . there's something empty in them.

Victor comes back out of the office and I glance up.

"I'm going to be clearing out Mom's locker at work," he tells me. "I'll bring her personal things home so you and Daisy can go through them. See if there's anything you want."

I nod, though my brain immediately starts spinning. A locker at work. Personal things. Surely, Mom wouldn't have kept anything questionable at the FBI, would she?

Chapter Four

"ZACH!" I CALL OUT THE NEXT DAY IN THE
school parking lot.

He turns around, and I leave Daisy by the Jeep.

He zips his jacket against the cold as he watches me
approach. "What's up?"

"I have a favor."

"This is new."

True. Reggie's the only one I ever ask favors of. "Mind taking Daisy out?"

Zach just looks at me.

"I mean, as a friend. That's all. She hasn't gone out since,
well, everything, and it would be good for her to be with some
friends again." *It would be good for her to not be trailing me.*

"Oh. Well, I suppose. But wouldn't her *real* friends be better at this?"

I glance around the student parking lot at the more-than-inquisitive gazes we're getting. The gossip surrounding all of us has been ridiculous. "Yes, but she doesn't want to be with them. She doesn't feel . . . safe."

"And she'll feel safe with me?"

"Yes, I believe so."

He glances over my shoulder to where Daisy is standing and looking at us. "All right. Tell her movie tonight. I'll pick her up at six."

I haven't touched him in months, so when I reach out and grasp his arm, it takes us both by surprise. So much surprise I lose what I want to say.

His dark eyes hold steady to mine as he waits. But when I don't say anything, he quietly prompts, "Lane?"

I blink and let go and take a step back. *Get ahold of yourself, Lane.* "Thanks, Zach. This means a lot to me. You taking Daisy out," I clarify.

He nods, and I ignore the urge to touch him again as I turn and walk back to Daisy. But as I walk, I have the distinct sensation he's still standing there, watching *over* me. Warmth settles through me at just the thought. *Over* me. That comforts me more than it should. And confuses me. I've never needed anybody watching over me.

To my surprise, Daisy doesn't fight it when I get back into the Jeep.

"Zach."

"Yep," I say as I crank the engine and heater.

"What about Dad and dinner?"

"He'll be fine." Actually, he'll probably be relieved. He could use a break. "Zach said he'd pick you up tonight at six." At 6:01 I'll be out the door and heading to Aisha. She and I are going to have a little talk.

We get Justin, head home, and do the usual snack/homework thing. At five minutes before six Zach rings our doorbell.

Justin answers. "Hi!"

Zach fist-bumps him. "Hey, little man. Daisy ready?"

"Daisy," Justin calls upstairs as Zach steps into our house.

The last time he was here, we were alone and having sex. Seems like an eternity ago now.

He turns and catches sight of me on my laptop at the dining room table. "Hey, you."

The warmth from earlier creeps back in, and my lips automatically curl up in response. I do love how he greets me. "Hey."

Daisy comes down the stairs dressed in jeans, a sweater, and boots. She's let her blond hair go naturally wavy and wears just a bit of makeup. I like the new Daisy. Not fake anymore. It's perplexing to me how tragedy changes people. She's becoming the sister I always wished I had. Minus the two peas thing.

I, however, have turned into an unfocused mess. But, hopefully, that will change tonight. With Aisha.

"You look nice," I honestly tell her.

She grins—"Thanks"—and turns to Zach. "Ready?"

"I was thinking Justin might want to come too?" Zach suggests.

Justin gives an excited little hop. "Really?"

Daisy takes one look at him and immediately softens. "Sure. Go ask Dad."

Wow, my sister really has changed.

Justin bolts into the office and seconds later comes back out. "He said yes!" He grabs his coat and they're all out the door. I don't get one last look from Zach and find myself disappointed with this.

I duck my head in the office. "Did you bring that stuff home of Mom's?"

"No, not yet." He glances up from his file. "Hey, with your brother and sister both gone, mind if we just fend for ourselves tonight?"

I smile. I knew he needed a break. "No problem. Can I do my usual coffee shop thing?"

"Sure, but why didn't you go with Zach too?"

It's not like him to question me, and it takes me off guard. "Big paper due tomorrow."

He nods. "All right."

"I'll be back by curfew," I tell him.

By six fifteen I'm in my Jeep and heading to Aisha's apartment in Alexandria. Her community is three-story, brick, and clean.

There are a lot of kids out in the common area playing, laughing, and I wonder if she has sold to any of them. Has approached any of them.

A couple walks by, pushing a baby stroller and shooting me a smile.

An older gentleman comes out of his apartment to check the mail.

Someone on the first floor opens a window, and I catch the faint sound of a kitchen smoke alarm beeping.

Seems like such a family-friendly complex for a drug dealer to live in.

Slowly I pull past the landing that leads to her second-story apartment, and Aisha walks right down the stairs. Perfect timing. She's dressed in all black and doesn't look up as she climbs into a dark car, backs up, and drives right past me out of the complex.

I do a U-turn and begin following at a safe distance.

She doesn't go far, pulling into a Starbucks. I park farther down the block and watch as she jumps out. Her dark hair is pulled back into a tight ponytail, like it was in Penn's court, and she wears tiny black-framed glasses.

Carrying an iPad, she pays a meter and goes inside the café.

If she did see me in the alley with Jacks, she wouldn't recognize me. I had my full-face mask on. So I don't worry as I cut my engine, wrap a scarf around my neck, and "talk" into my cell phone as I walk toward the Starbucks. To any onlooker I'm just another teen out for a caffeine fix and certainly not following someone.

Aisha's over in the corner, nibbling on a pastry and sliding her finger over her iPad. I take my place in line, and when it's my turn, I get my usual. Grande dark roast with room for milk.

At the cream stand I top it off with milk and, blowing on it, wander over to the magazine rack. I choose one with Kate Middleton on the front and pick a spot far enough away from Aisha but from which I can watch her.

I open my magazine and pretend to browse, all the while watching her study her iPad. I've already seen her in action selling to kids, but after Jacks being beaten, I want more of a sense of her and if she's capable of that type of violence. I take in her dark jeans and hoodie again. She's not as tall as me, but add a mask and she could easily be mistaken for the Masked Savior.

From my research I know she's younger than Jacks. Only nineteen. She got kicked out of her home and has been living with a friend for a few months. As nonthreatening as she looks with her glasses and ponytail, she's actually ideal for introducing young kids to drugs.

I take a final sip of coffee, close my magazine, glance one last time in her direction, and see her staring right at me.

I pause. There's no way she knows who I am.

She doesn't smile, just stares at me, and it sends a very distinct shiver of awareness across my neck. She's malicious. Of this I'm sure. If there's one thing I've developed, it's an intuition when it comes to evil, and Aisha just officially put mine on full alert.

Yes, she's capable of impersonating me and beating up Jacks. I'm sure of it.

Chapter Five

MOM GIVES ME A TENDERIZING MALLET.

"I want you to beat that chicken into submission," she jokes.

I tentatively start hammering it.

"Harder," she encourages.

I do.

"Harder," she reassures in a voice turned raspy and deep.

And I do.

Afterward she pats me on my shoulder. "Good girl. We'll try that again sometime."

I push the unwanted memory away and concentrate on prepping the coffeepot. I used to make French press all the time, but haven't in months. That had been mine and Mom's thing.

Grabbing the remote, I flip on the morning news. At the bottom is:

MASKED SAVIOR TARGETS PROSTITUTE

What?

Apparently last night "I" tasered, zip-tied, and beat up a prostitute. A prostitute? Give me a break. I wouldn't do that.

They found her near death in a Dumpster around midnight with a note left by the Masked Savior.

I don't leave notes.

Well, not normally. I did leave a note with Marco, the animal abuser, but that was different. I had to let people know my reasoning behind his torture.

But this? Why would "I" target a prostitute? Other than making decisions I personally wouldn't make, I have no beef with hookers.

MASKED SAVIOR TARGETS PROSTITUTE

I clench my jaw. As if my life isn't complicated enough, this news sucks so much frustrating ass.

Aisha. I get that she would've done Jacks in some sort of drug-deal partnership gone bad, but why would she attack this prostitute? Unless the prostitute was one of their clients, though I thought they targeted only kids. I followed Aisha to Starbucks and then left. She could've done this prostitute afterward.

I grab my laptop and bring the report up. Quickly I scan it. The prostitute was only fifteen. *Jesus.* That age makes sense with Aisha, though. I keep scanning. They do suspect drug play. She was found in Georgetown. I followed Aisha in Alexandria, so she could've easily gone from the coffee shop to Georgetown.

If Aisha impersonated me and did Jacks and now this prostitute, then she could very well be on the Masked Savior website and a member of my following. I click over to "my" site and scroll new comments.

[JellyJam] 15? Come on!

[Guapo0346] I don't get it. Why not just kill the prostitute?

[TurtleDove] Do you think the M.S. sleeps in a cape?

I scroll through the other comments and nothing jumps out at me. Of course if Aisha were on this site, her username wouldn't be Aisha.

First Jacks and now this new bludgeoning. With the news recently mentioning the URL, I'm sure site traffic has picked up.

My brother and sister come downstairs, ready to go. School is the last thing I want to do right now. All I can focus on is tonight and seeing Aisha again.

. . .

It's Daisy's turn to do the dishes, and this time I don't volunteer. Instead I grab my keys and am out the door.

When I'm a few blocks away from our home, I notice headlights behind me. I take a few turns just to see, and sure enough, the headlights keep pace. It's a dark car. And although I can't make out the gender of the person, through the mix of lights and shadows I can tell there's only one individual in the car.

I turn left onto Kirby. The car follows.

About a mile down, I hang a right on Westmoreland. The car does as well. *What the hell?*

Right on Haycock. So does the car.

I gun my engine, race right through a yellow light, and stare in my rearview mirror. The car stops.

I cut my lights, pull over into a condo community, and park behind a tree. I watch the road, waiting, waiting for the car, but don't see it.

There's no way I'm being paranoid. That car *was* following me. I pull out and backtrack, looking now for the car, but don't see anything.

Dark car. Aisha drives a dark one.

I glance at my watch: 8:50. If I head straight to her apartment, I wonder if I'll actually find her there.

My phone dings. It's Victor. WHERE ARE YOU?

Shit. I forgot to tell him I was leaving. SORRY, I quickly type back. RAN TO CVS. NEED ANYTHING?

NO. COMING HOME SOON?

I want to head over to Aisha's apartment, but it's obvious Victor is getting annoyed with my nightly outings. YES, I type back.

When I go away to college, this won't be an issue. But for now I need to go home and make a family appearance.

When I walk inside, Victor is in the living room watching CNN.

He swerves his eyes over to me, then down to my empty hands. "Thought you went to CVS?"

Damn. *Before* Mom I wouldn't have made this mistake. "It's in the car. Just some supplies I need for school."

Justin comes racing down the stairs. "Lane! You're home."

Daisy steps out of the laundry room and smiles. "Hi."

Have I really been this absent from my family? I look at each of them as guilt nestles its annoying little self inside me. Yes, I have been absent. I always have. Before Mom it never seemed an issue, though.

I head over and take a seat on the couch with Victor. I want to ask him again if he brought home Mom's personal stuff from the office but don't want to seem too eager. I'll give it another couple of days, and then I'll ask him.

Justin plops down beside me, and we all silently watch

the headlines. I think we must be the only household with twenty-four/seven news playing. With both my parents in the FBI, it sort of goes with the territory.

A few minutes in, Daisy brings a basket of laundry over and starts folding it.

One look and anyone would peg us as normal.

Victor flips the channel to a local one, and I tune in to what a commentator is saying. "Another child has overdosed. Something needs to be done. This one was only ten. Find who's giving these kids drugs and put them in jail. Is it really that hard?"

Daisy sighs. "That's horrible. Giving drugs to a kid. Ten years old? God!"

I look over to my brother. He'll be ten in a couple of years.

The mother of the child comes on the TV, crying, pleading with anyone who might know who gave her child drugs.

I'll never understand how people deal with death. The crying. I haven't shed a tear since I killed my mother. I suppose I'm more of a weep-on-the-inside type of griever. Then again, I'm not really grieving. My mother deserved to die.

Who am I kidding? I *am* grieving. I miss the mother I thought she was. And I'm confused and angry and frustrated at how she tricked me, my brother, my sister, my stepdad. How she tricked all of us into thinking she was this great mom.

Yeah, I'm really effing pissed about that.

Something loosens inside me. Like a dawning realization. Why has it taken me three months to realize this? To realize I'm pissed at her for betraying all of us.

Victor looks down at my brother. "Justin, you know never to take things from strangers, right? Never."

Justin nods. "Yeah, Dad."

"Please," the mother continues on-screen, "if anyone knows anything . . ."

I have no idea if Aisha is responsible for this boy, but I do know she's a link that needs to be severed.

"Lane, you got a card in the mail," Victor tells me. "It's on the dining room table."

I walk over to see a yellow Hallmark envelope. It's not my birthday, so I know it's another one of those ridiculous "Sorry for your loss" cards. I don't want to open it, but because my family is in the same room, I pull the thick yellow card out, ignore the dove embossed on the front, and open it.

It says simply:

Your mom was loved by many.

No signature. No return address. But the postmark reads Richmond.

"Who's it from?" Victor asks.

"Just someone from school," I automatically lie. "They moved to Richmond," I follow up, in case he looked at the envelope.

I don't know anyone who lives in Richmond. This has got to be someone who knew my mom. But why send this to just me? Why not send it to the whole family?

Chapter Six

DAISY SLEEPS WITH ME THAT NIGHT, AND IN the morning I tentatively start, "Daisy, I think it's important you start sleeping by yourself."

Across the pillows her eyes go wide. "Why? Have I done something wrong?"

Her panic deflates me a little. "It's just that Dr. Depof said part of healing involves each of us taking independent steps."

I climb out of my bed and trudge over to my desk, where I left my water bottle. I take a few gulps, if anything to give me a second. "I was proud of the way you and Justin went out with Zach."

Normally I don't say this type of thing, but it seems to be all that comes to me.

She sits up in bed, and I swear she's about to cry. "Well, if I'm cramping your style . . ."

I close my eyes. *Lane, be nice to your sister.* "No, you're not cramping my style," I outright lie.

"Well then, what is it?"

I channel Dr. Depof's words. "Like I said, healing involves independent steps." I fake a loving laugh. "Just trying to exert some tough love." And actually, I suppose I really am.

She looks away, and I hope beyond hope she's deciding to indeed take those independent steps. "Maybe just a few more days?"

Inside, I sigh. "Okay. A few more days."

"Thanks, Lane. You really are the best sister."

Despite all the crap going on inside me, I know she's right. I am a good sister. Or at least I try to be.

I head downstairs, and while I'm making coffee, I flip on the news.

ANOTHER MASKED SAVIOR VICTIM

Jesus!

This one took place in Silver Spring, Maryland, last night. I've never been to Silver Spring. A homeless teen was found tasered, zip-tied, and beaten to near death by a baseball bat. Drugs are suspected to be involved. Witnesses report a person dressed in all black and a ski mask who can be none other than the Masked Savior.

It occurred at ten in the evening. If Aisha was in that dark car following me last night that was between eight thirty and nine. She could've made it to Silver Spring and committed this act.

The one thing I do know—it wasn't me.

Drugs suspected. Teen boy. Sounds like Aisha.

The reporter goes on to detail a local task force that has been put together to blanket DC and the surrounding areas to stop the Masked Savior from continuing this string of violence.

Great. Now I have a task force hunting "my" ass.

I grab my laptop and bring up "my" site. Sure enough the message board is buzzing.

[underground_jill] Homeless teen? Give me a break!

[mean-liz] Do u really think the M.S. did this?

[j_d_l] M.S. should be targeting whoever gave that 10-yr-old drugs.

My thoughts exactly. Wait a minute, j_d_l left a comment before, too. I scroll back through the pages and find his other post. *The M. Savior should've overdosed JJJ like he did those kids.*

I agreed with him then, too. I'm not sure I like that I agree with someone on my forum.

Victor comes out of the office and lays an unopened card on the dining room table. It's another condolence. This one's pale blue. I hate these cards.

"Just put it with the others," he tells me, and I know he hates them too.

I pick it up, see it's postmarked Richmond as well, and open it. It's the same handwriting, but this time addressed solely to Victor:

My thoughts are with you and the children in this tragic time. ~Marji

"From someone named Marji," I say. "Who's that?"

He gives that some thought, then shrugs. "I don't know. Probably someone your mom knew from work. Just put it with the others," he says again.

Marji. I roll that name around in my head. I don't recall my mom ever speaking about a Marji. And why would she send me a card and then Victor one too? That doesn't make any sense.

I slip it under my laptop and head to my Saturday shift at Patch and Paw. I'll see if I can figure out this Marji puzzle later. This Masked Savior copycat comes first.

When I get to the animal hospital, I find Corn Chip in his usual spot. "Hey, C-squared."

He does that whole-body-wiggle thing and I melt. I love the little guy. I let him out and pick a few other dogs he likes better than the rest. We all go out to the side yard. I throw ten too many balls and smile as they yip-yap their way in a zillion different directions trying to get them all.

"If Corn Chip's mom ever decides to give him up, you'll be first in line to adopt."

I don't have to turn around to know Dr. Issa's behind me. "True."

He takes a step closer and I close my eyes. There's something about Dr. Issa that always stirs my insides.

"You missed a great surgery earlier," he says. "Wished you could've been here."

"What was it?"

"Open heart on a German shepherd."

I turn around, my momentary pleasure replaced by genuine curiosity. "How *was* it?"

Dr. Issa smiles. "Phenomenal." And then he goes on to describe in detail all that was done.

He finishes and I'm totally jealous. "Next time try to wait for me to scrub in. Please."

He nods. "I will." Neither one of us says anything for a few seconds, and then he tilts his head and gives me a study. "How you holding up, Lane?"

I've always found it difficult to lie to Dr. Issa. My guard seems even more down around him since killing Mom. "Pretty shitty," I honestly tell him.

His lips curve in amused understanding. "Great description."

He lost his mom years ago. Granted, he didn't kill her, but at least he knows what it's like to lose a mom.

"Would you like to talk?" he offers.

"No." I shrug. "It felt good just saying that much." Actually, it feels really damn good.

"Okay." His phone buzzes, and right before he answers, he says, "Know I'm here anytime if you change your mind."

"Thanks."

He heads off, and I do my usual shift. At the end I make my way into the medical closet and straight over to the tranquilizer section. I snag a vial off the shelf in preparation for Aisha.

I sign out, hop on the parkway, and take it all the way to her apartment community. In a spot not illuminated by a streetlamp, I parallel park a little up from her door. I sit for a second and take things in. She's home. I see her car.

I do one last visual sweep of the area and get out my science homework. I try to read but it's too dark. Plus my thoughts are scattered. I close my eyes and play through the scenarios of how this might unfold. If Aisha leaves tonight, she could go to Starbucks again. But I can't go inside. She's already seen me once. A second sighting will be way too suspicious.

For all I know, she could already be out with one of her drug pals beating someone up in my name and have left her car at home. I open my eyes to check my watch at the exact second my driver's door flies open and someone yanks me from my Jeep.

A *huge* guy pushes me up against my hood. "Who are you?" He gives me a hard shove. "What do you want?"

Fear slams into me and my whole body uncontrollably shakes.

Don't succumb to weakness or inferiority. I try my best to channel my aikido sensei's words but come up blank as I stare up into the man's narrow black eyes. What is *wrong* with me?

Into my peripheral vision steps Aisha. I swallow, and way back in my brain echoes, *You're in trouble.*

"Why are you following me?" she quietly asks.

I try to speak but am rendered mute.

She steps closer. "I. Said. Why. Are. You. Following. Me?"

I swallow again. "I'm not."

Her eyes narrow. "Let this be a warning. I catch you again, and you'll wish you never saw my face." She raises her dark brows. "Got it?"

I manage a jerky nod.

Aisha reaches forward and pinches my earlobe. "Got it?"

"Yes," I croak.

Big guy grabs the front of my jacket and shoves me back in my Jeep. They stand there while I fumble with my key, jab it in the ignition, grind the car in gear, and pull away. I don't look back once, and only after I'm *several* miles down the road do I pull over and release the death grip I have on my steering wheel.

I gulp in a couple of breaths as my heart bangs in my chest

cavity. Holy shit in good goddamn hell. I haven't felt so alive in months.

I put my fingers to the artery in my neck and feel it pulsing my pads, and my mind zings back through the years. . . .

Screams shatter the air. Blood splatters the ceiling.

Mom rears the knife above her head and lunges toward the woman.

Dad turns to me, delight dancing in his eyes. "Is your heart pounding? Do you feel how alive this makes you?"

Chapter Seven

THE NEXT NIGHT AS I'M HEADING TO HAVE a little one-on-one Taser/zip-tie conversation with Aisha, Victor announces, "Wait right there. We're going to church tonight."

Daisy, Justin, and I all look at each other. I can't remember the last time we went to church, and, clearly, neither can my brother and sister.

I hold up my book bag. "I was heading to—"

"No, you're not. There's a service tonight. Thirty minutes," he tells us, and heads into his room to get ready.

I don't disguise my aggravated sigh.

Forty-five minutes later we're walking into McLean Worship Center. It's packed, and we find seats in the church equivalent of the nosebleed section. No one spares us a glance, and I find the anonymity comforting.

The sermon is on breaking free from the past. I chance a quick look up at heaven. Did God know I was going to be here today?

The minister is saying, "As we focus and put on our new self, we will obtain freedom from that which has shackled us. Colossians . . ."

Freedom from that which has shackled us. Why didn't I see this before? I need to release my mom and my dad. I need to say good-bye and let their ghosts go.

All these childhood memories I've been having. Taking my energies out on that cheerleader and that freshman. Freezing up with Jacks. Being taken off guard by Aisha. I've lost my focus. I need to get it back.

Officially saying good-bye to my parents is the key to regaining my equilibrium and purpose.

The sermon continues and I listen intently. Maybe this church thing isn't so bad after all. By nine o'clock we're back home, and I go straight to my room.

I clear it of anything that is connected to my mom. The necklace she gave me when I was ten, the books she bought me at twelve, and the souvenirs she picked up when on business trips. Everything I can find, I gather it and put it in box.

I crank up my laptop and delete every picture and every file of not only her as my mom, but the Decapitator as well. I don't ever want to see anything again.

When I come downstairs, Victor shoots me a look. "Where are you going?"

I hold the box up. "My lab partner texted me that he needs this stuff. Mind if I make a quick run?"

He nods. "Okay, be safe."

"I will." I stop. Now would be a good time to ask. "Did you ever clear out Mom's personal stuff from her locker?" If he did, I could dispose of it, too.

"No."

I nod. I know it's hard on him. I'll be patient.

He sighs. "But I will. This week. I promise."

"Take your time," I encourage him, and he gives me a relieved smile.

I'm out the door and driving to a gas station to fill up an empty gallon container. I jump on the toll road and go straight to where it all started—4 Buchold Place in Herndon.

I sit in the yard for a few seconds remembering when I came here with my mom. She walked through the house with me, acting all normal, knowing what she and my father had done here. Knowing what they made me watch. What they made me participate in.

Anger rolls through me, heating me to a boil, making my jaw clench and my breath come slower, deeper.

I hate her. I hate him. I hate what they did to me. What they made me become.

I throw my door open, stalk to the house, and use my keys to let myself in. I go straight to the room where they killed my preschool teacher and stand in the center, panting now, seething, allowing the raging fury in. To take over.

I toss the box of mementos down, saturate the whole room with gas from the container, and open the window.

I charge straight out the front door, pull a lighter from my pocket, flick it, lock it, and throw it in through the ajar window. The room erupts in flames, and my pulse deepens to a thick thud.

I stand for a second, watching, soaking the heat into my face as the flames cleanse me. Renew me. I am my parents' daughter. I am a killer. But I am *nothing* like them. Nor will I ever be. I will *not* carry on their twisted legacy.

I am me. I am justified.

A siren pierces the air and I move, not even glancing back as I pull away. I don't have enough time to fit an Aisha visit in, so I drive straight home to find Daisy waiting in my room.

"I'm ready to 'part ways,'" she tells me.

"Excuse me?"

She laughs a little and it reminds me of the old Daisy. "I'm ready to be a big girl again. I'm moving back into my room.

And I'm going to start eating lunch with my friends again. No more bugging you."

"You weren't bugging me," I fib.

She rolls her eyes. "Yes, I was."

I smile. "Well, just don't go back to being a bitch."

Daisy gives me a playful punch.

"Hey!"

And then she wraps her arms around me. "I love you, Lane."

I hug her back, harder than I recall ever hugging her before. "I love you, too."

She heads out and I sit on the edge of my bed. It seems that sermon did us all some good.

Victor knocks on my door.

"Come in."

He hands me a business card. "Listen, I know you don't like Dr. Depof. So I'm hereby giving you permission to not go anymore."

I almost fall over in shock, but glance at the business card instead. "What's this?"

"It's a group thing. Thought you might like that better. If you go, it'd be just you going, no family. It's a mixture of people who have lost loved ones."

Yes, but is it a mixture of people who have *killed* their loved ones? "Do you want me to go?"

"I would very much like that, but I'll leave the ultimate decision up to you."

I look up into his caring eyes and see how much this means to him. "Okay, I'll give it a try."

He smiles, and my heart relaxes at his relief. "Good night, then."

"Good night, Dad."

He turns back. "I really love it when you call me Dad. Thank you for that."

Mom always insisted I call him Victor. She was adamant he was my stepfather. I never realized it until now, but I bet that hurt him. And it gives me one more reason to despise her.

From now on I will always call Victor Dad. Because the truth is, he's more of a parent than my real ones ever were.

Chapter Eight

THE NEXT MORNING DURING FIRST BLOCK TA, Zach finds me in the library. "Hey, you."

"Hey."

"Can we talk?"

In my experience that question rarely prefaces a positive conversation. "Okay."

He blows out a nervous breath that makes me even more curious as to what he wants to say. "We haven't really *talked*-talked since everything happened, and I was hoping we could have a little heart-to-heart."

I give him my full attention.

He pulls the chair out beside me and takes a seat. "It's not a big secret that I had the world's biggest crush on you."

I catch the word "had." And . . . "crush"? I wouldn't call what we had a crush. We had sex. That qualifies as more than a crush in my mind, but I continue listening.

"The thing is, I like you. Sometimes I like you too much. And that freaks me out. Especially with our history."

Is he talking about me beating up his ex-girlfriend, Belinda? Or maybe he's talking about the fact he was strapped naked to a table, about to be killed, and my mom "rescued" him.

"I keep thinking we can maybe get back to where we were or pick up where we left off or whatever, but it's not going to work. I've discussed this with my therapist, and that's why I'm here talking to you. I'm choosing honesty over avoidance."

Everyone seems to have a therapist these days.

"Have you thought about this at all?" he asks.

No, not really. I don't reply with this, though, and instead am brutally honest. "Zach, I like you. I trust you. But I don't want to date you." I *can't* date anybody. I have way too much going on inside this bizarre head of mine. "I do, however, want another orgasm."

His face turns slightly red.

I shrug. "Just being honest."

He laughs a little. "That right there is why I fell so hard for you from the get-go. However, my services are not for hire."

I give his joke a smile. "I get that."

We stare at each other for a few long seconds as his laughter gradually fades away. Something in the air shifts between us, making me wonder what he's going to say next.

He sighs and looks away. "I don't want to be friends. I mean, I want to, but I can't. I'm sorry." He brings his eyes back to mine. "Please don't ask me to do you any more favors. I don't want to be mean to you; I'll acknowledge you when I see you, but I don't want to talk anymore. This is something I have to do for me and my recovery. And I'm going to tell Daisy not to call me anymore too."

Recovery? He hasn't gone back to drinking, has he? "Zach . . ." Wow, I'm speechless.

He stands. "Maybe someday . . ." He gives his head a quick shake. "No. I'm getting sidetracked, *again*, which is so easy to do with you. Okay, see you around."

I watch him walk back across the library, and with each step emptiness knocks around inside me. *I don't want to be friends.* I'm floored. I can't believe he actually said that.

But . . . I get it. I wish I didn't, but I do. He knows what he needs to do to heal—to move on. It sucks that it's staying away from me. But, yeah, I get it.

The question is: What do *I* need?

I need to stop Aisha and this copycat thing. I also need to find out who Marji is.

• • •

That night I find my stepdad in the office looking through all the condolence cards I had put away. His sad expression sends a pang through my heart. "You okay?" I quietly ask.

He closes the latest one, the one from that Marji woman. "Yes, fine." He gives me a fake smile. "Heading out?"

I hesitate. Yes, I want to, but maybe he needs me here.

"Go," he encourages me, seemingly reading my mind. "Everything's fine."

I still hesitate.

"Seriously." He laughs a little. "Go."

"Okay . . . but can I borrow your car? My heater's not working too well." Plus, Aisha won't know me in his car.

"Oh, well, let's make sure we get it checked."

He gives me his keys, I grab my supplies from my Jeep, and I'm off to Alexandria and Aisha's apartment. Except all the way there I can only think about Victor's sad expression. Sometimes I wish I could just tell him how Mom really was so he wouldn't be so lost without her.

About an hour into sitting, thinking, and waiting, Aisha comes out of her apartment alone, and my pulse spikes with nervous excitement. She's dressed in all black and has a beanie on.

Here we go, copycat.

She glances around as she makes her way to her car. I let her get a few blocks ahead and slowly begin to follow. With her nondescript car, she's not easy to trail, and I nearly lose her a time or two. I'm assured, though, between the traffic and Victor's car, there's no way she can know I'm following her. She takes the parkway all the way to where it dumps out near Langley and heads into Falls Church from there. She pulls into a neighborhood with nut-to-butt Cape Cods and parks along the curb.

I go right past her, out for a merry little drive, take a left, and park behind a playground where some middle school kids are playing a late-night game of soccer on the frozen field. I get out my binoculars, and as I focus in on her image, my heart picks up pace. She has no clue I'm watching her, and that one fact alone has my lips curving up in satisfaction.

Tonight's the night, Aisha.

I watch her as she scopes out the kids. The playground. The soccer game. The surroundings.

I lower my binoculars and study the same scene.

She opens her door and climbs out. She crosses to the playground and sits in the darkness under a tree. A couple of the middle school boys glance her way. What is she up to?

I look around at the surrounding houses. The parents probably think this a great little neighborhood. Their kids can play. They can glance out through their windows and check on them. Call them home from their front doors. Safe.

Nothing is safe. Don't people understand that?

A few of the boys head home. Now there's just a couple

left. They seem older. Maybe thirteen or fourteen. They glance Aisha's way before looking around and then slowly heading over. I can't hear what they're saying, but they're standing in front of her. One has a soccer ball tucked under his arm. The other one holds a dark plastic water bottle.

He hands it to her. She unscrews the top and glances inside, then reaches into her hoodie pocket, pulls out a similar bottle, and hands that one to him.

They've got this thing down pat. I'd bet anything there's money in the first bottle and drugs in the other.

The boy doesn't look inside, and instead he and his buddy head off.

She remains sitting, watching them walk away. I lower my ski mask and slip from Victor's car. I slide the tranquilizer gun into my side cargo pocket and, in the darkness, I make my way toward her.

She has no clue I'm here. I can have her tasered and zip-tied in under a minute. For that matter I can shoot her with my tranquilizer gun and be done with her. But then she'd be left for dead, propped against the tree, to be found frozen in the morning.

Plus, what good is that going to do me? I want some answers. I want to know about Jacks and the prostitute and the homeless boy. I want to know why she was following me the other night and why she's copycatting me.

I continue hovering in the shadows, eyeing her, waiting, enjoying the throbbing in my blood that the anticipation brings. My ears tune in to the stillness of the night. Winter always seems to make everything quieter.

She gets up and makes her way through the empty playground, out the other side, and back toward her car.

I follow.

With one last glance up and down the dark street, I go to raise my Taser at the same second she opens her door, catches sight of my reflection in the glass, and whips around.

Immediately I move, lunging, ramming the heel of my hand into the tip of her nose. Her head snaps back, she slips, falls into her doorjamb, and loses consciousness.

I take in a breath and hold it as I stare down at her unconscious body. What the . . . ?

Goddamnit.

I give her body a jab with my boot. She's out. And I have no answers.

With a sigh I do another quick survey of the empty street. I don't zip-tie her. I don't want this connected to the Masked Savior.

I pick her up and shove her in her car, and as I do, I catch sight of a baseball bat in her backseat. Jacks, the teen prostitute, the homeless boy—they were all beaten with a bat.

Looks like I was right about Aisha being my copycat.

I search her pockets and find all kinds of drugs. I dig through her glove box and find the same. I don't bother looking anywhere else. I'm sure she's got paraphernalia tucked everywhere.

Between the baseball bat, the drugs, and her dark outfit, the cops are going to get her on everything. *Slim justice.* They'll think they just nabbed the Masked Savior.

I find her phone, punch her one last time in the head to make sure she stays out, and dial 911. I toss the phone on the floorboard and truck it back to Victor's car. I wait to make sure she doesn't wake up, and when I hear sirens, I slowly leave the neighborhood.

This was what I needed. Righting a wrong. Defeating evil.

But other than the initial tingling in my blood, there were no pulsing arteries. No throbbing veins. No spiked adrenaline.

If this was what I needed, then how come it doesn't feel as great as I thought it would?

Chapter Nine

AISHA IS ALL OVER THE NEWS THE NEXT evening, and as I had hoped, there is heavy speculation she is the Masked Savior.

Good.

I bring up "my" site to see it buzzing.

[Omar_Fire] Give me a break. Aisha's not the M.S.

[MikeyMike] I agree!

[JaxcyOnyx] Will the real M.S. please stand up?

I sigh. No one on the forum believes Aisha and the Masked Savior are one and the same.

[j_d_l] M.S. should've tranq'd her. It's what Aisha deserved.

I read and reread that line. *Tranq'd her.* I did have my tranquilizer gun out before I slipped it into my pocket. But the

Masked Savior is known for Taser and zip ties, not tranquilizer, because I've never used it.

Which means the only way j_d_l could've known about the tranquilizer gun is if he had been there. My heart skips a beat and I take in a shallow breath. He was there, watching me.

No.

Did I just waste my time on Aisha? Was she not the one following me, copycatting me? *No!* How did I not sense this other person? How did I not know there was someone hiding in the shadows?

This isn't good.

That means this person may know who I am. He may have seen me without my mask.

If I hadn't been so driven, I would've felt his presence. This isn't good at all and proves I have to be more alert. I have to be more on my game. Before Mom, I would've been.

Game. That word floats around in my head as an idea forms.

From an anonymous handle, I instant message j_d_l: WELCOME TO MY WORLD. ARE YOU SURE YOU WANT TO PLAY?

"I have some bad news."

I look up from my laptop and straight into Victor's eyes. "Oh?"

"Your father's place, the house you inherited, burned down," he tells me.

"Oh," I simply respond, though of course I already know this.

"Cops think it was some neighborhood kids playing around with gas and fire. Anyway, there's also a buyer. An elderly couple. Once the insurance company signs off, the buyers are going to clear the land and rebuild. Like your mom said, I'll put the money in your college account."

I nod. "Thanks."

"There will be some paperwork for you to sign since the house is in your name."

"Okay." Once that paperwork is signed, I'll officially be free of 4 Buchold Place. The most evil place I know.

"Are you going to that grief group I told you about?" he asks.

"Is that tonight?"

He gives me a patient look. "Yes."

Inside I sigh, but being the good daughter I pretend to be, I close everything down and grab my keys. "On my way," I tell him, when all I really want to do is wait for j_d_l's response.

I arrive to grief group a little late. There are twelve people in all, and as they introduce themselves, I discover they range in age from fifteen up to thirty. This one is considered the "young" group, and then there's a "mature" group that meets at a different time.

Across the circle from me sits a blond-haired guy I recognize. We went to middle school together, I think. He was in eighth grade when I was in seventh, which would make him a freshman in college now. That is, if he's in college.

He introduces himself. "My name is Tommy and I've been coming on and off for a while now. My sister died several months ago, and I'm just trying to find my way back."

"Welcome, Tommy," the counselor greets him.

"Welcome, Tommy," a few of the others parrot.

I don't say anything, but I do look at both of his arms covered in tats. To each their own, but I've never understood the concept of tattoos and piercings.

The introductions continue, and I only slightly listen as I think back to the news report on Aisha. She is in jail, being held without bond. They found enough drugs on her and in her car to put her away for a very long time. Plus with the bat and the way she was dressed, she's indeed the number one Masked Savior suspect.

At least she's locked up, and the streets are somewhat safer now—from drugs—but not from whoever was out there watching me.

"Hello?" the counselor prompts.

I blink and sit up, suddenly realizing everyone is staring at me. "Sorry."

The counselor raises his brows. "Would you like to introduce yourself?"

I clear my throat. "Lane. Seventeen. Mom's dead."

Everyone in the circle exchanges confused glances, and the grief counselor smiles warmly. "Welcome, Lane."

I don't smile back. "Thanks."

The group continues for an hour, talking about, hell, I don't know what. I don't bother listening. I don't need this crap to heal. What I need is to get out and figure out how this j_d_l guy factors into everything. If Aisha *wasn't* the one following me, *wasn't* the one copycatting me, then it's got to be this j_d_l person. Though I won't know for sure if Aisha is blameless unless another victim pops up.

Lastly there is Marji, this mysterious person from Richmond.

I think through all the things that need my focus, paying no attention to the meeting. Finally, the hour is up and I head out. As I'm unlocking my Jeep, headlights flip on down the road and a car slowly comes toward me.

I edge closer to my Jeep, giving the car room on the narrow street, and it slows to an almost crawl when it gets nearer. I glance over my shoulder, squinting against the headlights, and damn me, it's a dark car. Individual occupant. Same as before.

A streetlight catches the driver in a brief illumination. A woman. Black hair. But just as quickly as the light flashes on her face, it's gone, and she guns the engine and zips by. I whip around, try to read her tag, but can't make it out. It's a BMW, though.

I jump in my Jeep to follow, make it to the end of the street, hang a right, and can't find her. My gaze bounces over the taillights of the cars in front of me, but I don't see hers. I keep driving, searching, but don't see her BMW anywhere.

Are you j_d_l?

I didn't just imagine that, right? Dark car. Single occupant. But . . . maybe she was going slow so she wouldn't hit me. There're a lot of dark cars out there. There's nothing to say that's the same one as before. No, she *was* looking at me. In that brief flash of streetlight, she was looking at me. Or at least I thought she was.

I sigh. It's annoying doubting myself.

Dark blue BMW. I'll catalog that for now. If I see her again, I'll know for sure.

I drive on home to find Victor in the kitchen seemingly anticipating my return.

"How'd it go?" he asks before I close the door.

"You waiting on me?"

He nods. "And? Did you like it?"

"No. I doubt I'm going to go back."

His hopeful expression slowly fades, and in its place settles one of annoyance. "Everyone around here is trying but you. So you know what? Fine. Do whatever you want to do, Lane."

With that he grabs his glass of wine, walks into the office, and shuts the door.

I don't move, I'm so in shock. I can't recall him ever taking that agitated tone with me before. Ever. He's really pissed.

Everyone around here is trying but you.

That's not true. We all put out effort in our own way. It's just . . . they wouldn't understand *my* way. And I've been here for my brother and my sister. Hell, Daisy's been sleeping in my room for the past three months. Why didn't Victor give me credit for that?

Yes, I've been here for Daisy and Justin, but . . . I haven't really been here for my stepdad. No one has. If me going to this group helps him deal with all of this, then I need to go.

I walk to the office and knock on the door.

"Come in," he curtly says.

I open the door just enough to stick my head through. "I'm sorry. I really am. I was being selfish. I'll keep going back."

He spares me a very brief look. "Good."

I give it a couple more seconds, but neither of us says anything else, and so I close his door. Yes, Victor's pissed. But I'll go, and I'll participate, and I'll try to make him happy.

Chapter Ten

THE NEXT MORNING BEFORE I LEAVE FOR school, Victor hands me a couple of pictures. "I've been going through Mom's stuff. I found a few photos of your father, Seth. Thought you'd want them."

I swallow an uncharacteristic and very sudden nervous swell in my throat. It doesn't do any good and I force another swallow.

Pictures of Seth? No, no I don't want them. I purged myself of him. Of Mom.

Victor hands me the pictures, obviously not picking up on my hesitancy, and I do the only thing I can. I take them.

He walks off, and I'm left standing in the kitchen staring down at a photo of Mom and Seth, grinning, their arms wrapped around each other. They look happy. Innocent. Young. I flip it over and note the date. Before I was even born.

I look at the second picture. It must have been taken the same day because they're wearing identical clothes. But this one has a dark-haired woman in it. She looks young too. About the same age as them. They're all smiling, hugging each other. Something about her seems familiar. I flip the photo over and see the same date, as I thought.

"What are you looking at?" Daisy asks.

I look up from the photos to see Daisy and Justin ready for school and waiting. "Pictures of my real dad and our mom."

Daisy and Justin exchange a look. "Can we see?" Daisy asks.

"Sure." I hand them to her and watch their faces as they study the two pictures.

"You look a lot like your dad," Daisy tells me.

"And you look just like Mom," I reply.

"Who do I look like?" Justin asks.

"Dad," Daisy and I answer in unison, and we all smile at each other.

"Who's the other woman?" Justin asks.

I shrug. "A friend of theirs, I guess." I want to ask if she seems familiar but for some reason don't. "Well, you guys ready?"

They hand the pictures back, and we're out the door. When we get home, I'll ask Victor about that other woman and see if he knows her. Also, I want to know if the two pictures are from Mom's personal locker at work. And if so, what else is there?

Kyle, science club president, finds me at my school locker. "Hey, Slim."

I put a couple folders away and grab a few more. "What's up, Kyle?"

"My younger sister and your little brother both go to the same elementary school."

I nod. I know.

Kyle leans up against the locker beside me. "Has Justin mentioned anything about someone trying to sell him drugs?"

I turn to fully face him. "No. What are you talking about?"

Kyle puts his backpack down. "I walk my sister and her friend home from school nearly every day. They don't think I'm listening with my iPod in, but I've heard them mention this guy, Bucky. Apparently he's approached a few of the elementary kids."

"Why haven't they reported it?"

"Scared, I guess." He shrugs. "Probably threatening them not to say anything. I hate bullies."

I can imagine. I've seen Kyle get pushed around a few times.

"Anyway," he continues, "I just wanted to see if you knew anything. I'm going to talk to my parents tonight."

And I'm going to talk to Justin.

. . .

Which is exactly what I do when Daisy and I pick him up after school. "Who's Bucky?"

My brother's eyes go really wide. "How do you know Bucky?"

My inner sense flips to full alert. "Who is he?"

"He's Annie's brother."

"And Annie is?"

"A girl in my class."

Daisy looks between us. "Are you talking about Annie Holmstead?"

Justin nods. "Yeah, that's right. She lives in that colorful house."

By "colorful house" I know my brother means the green-and-purple historical one a few blocks from the elementary campus. Bucky Holmstead. I'm going to find this stupid Bucky, and I'm going to see what his deal is.

I drop Justin off at after-school tutoring and Daisy at her friend Samantha's house, and I circle back around to the neighborhood where the green-and-purple house sits.

I parallel park and check things out. People come and go from the surrounding homes, but there's no movement from the colorful one. A few minutes in and I get out my iPhone and type in *Bucky Holmstead, Falls Church, Virginia*.

I get about a dozen hits.

The guy's eighteen. Most recent arrest was for drug possession and assault with a baseball bat. *Baseball bat.* I pull his picture up. And pause.

Well, hello there. It's the guy who yanked me out of my Jeep at Aisha's house. How *lovely* our paths should cross again.

I continue scrolling through links, reading. I'm sure he's got a juvie record, although that won't be public knowledge. For the kids not to have reported Bucky, he must really have them scared. Hell, he scared me.

I agree with Kyle; bullies rank right up there with how bad I loathe animal abusers.

I give the house one last look before putting my Jeep in gear and driving off. I'm going to get home, grab my laptop, and really dig in to researching this Bucky guy. Drugs. Baseball bat. Knows Aisha. This just might be my link to figuring out who was watching me the other night.

But when I get home, Victor's in the office. I'd forgotten this was his work-from-home day. He's with someone. I hear "Masked Savior" and purposefully hang in the dining room to eavesdrop.

"I appreciate you letting me pick your brain," the visitor is saying.

"Hey, listen, we made it through fifteen years in the army together. Letting you pick my brain is the least."

"While we didn't condone it, this vigilante used to be

harmless. Hell, he did our job for us. But now with the recent bludgeonings, he's morphed into a danger to society."

Well, shit. Does this mean they don't think Aisha is the Masked Savior?

"What's the local task force put together so far?" Victor asks.

"We've combed the streets, upped surveillance, and come up empty. There's a website we've been keeping tabs on," the man continues.

"That's a good strategy," Victor says.

Well, shit again. I should've already thought of that—I would've before. If they're monitoring the site, they can track the IP addresses of those who have posted. I IM'd j_d_l. My IP address is officially traceable now.

"What's your gut telling you?" Victor asks.

The man chuckles. "Exact reason why I'm here. I want to know if I'm crazy or not before I take this hypothesis to the task force."

"Go ahead."

"I think—"

"Hello."

I spin around to see a girl standing behind me. "Who are you?" I ask.

She sticks her hand out. "I'm Catalina." She nods to the office. "My dad is in there with your dad."

I shake her hand. "Where'd you come from?"

"I've been sitting over there in the corner reading a magazine." She grins. "Watching you eavesdrop."

I don't bother denying it and in fact admire her boldness. I give her a solid look. Tall like me and even skinnier. Wavy dark hair. Cool gray eyes. I'd say about sixteen.

Our fathers walk from the office, and I squash my irritation. I barely got a chance to hear anything at all.

"Don't worry," she whispers, "I won't tell them you were listening in."

I don't respond.

"Oh, hey, Lane, this is an army pal of mine. Mr. Coffey."

We shake hands.

"I heard you talking about the Masked Savior?" I say.

This earns a laugh from Catalina. She hadn't expected me to dime out my own eavesdropping self.

"Yes, Mr. Coffey's on the local task force," Victor answers. "We were discussing some scenarios."

What scenarios? I want to ask, since Catalina annoyingly interrupted me listening in.

Mr. Coffey looks between us. "You girls have heard of this Masked Savior thing, I'm sure."

We both nod.

"You two be alert and safe when you're out and about, okay?"

We nod again.

Catalina gives me an amused grin as they leave. What's so effing funny? The Masked Savior task force is in *my* house talking to *my* stepdad about me. This is so far from funny I don't even know where to start.

I turn to Victor. "Are you going to be on the task force too?" God, I hope not.

He shakes his head. "No, this isn't FBI jurisdiction. I was just giving advice. Friend to friend." He nods to the office. "Sorry, conference call in five. See you later for dinner."

I nod, grab a Coke from the refrigerator, and head straight up to my room. The first thing I do is go to "my" site, delete the unanswered message I sent j_d_l, and take my registration down. I know they can still pull up a ghost image of my IP address, but at least now I can honestly say I *was* a member, curious like so many others, and then took my registration down after I realized the ridiculousness of the whole thing.

What a mess.

I do some more queries on the task force and basically get what the news has already given. What I heard Mr. Coffey say. Upped surveillance. Combing the streets.

I need to lure j_d_l out and see what his connection is to all this. Plus there's Bucky. If I'm lucky, they are one and the same and I can officially put this whole copycat thing to rest. Though that still doesn't explain the woman in the dark car.

Chapter Eleven

"THERE'S LIKE THIS TINGLING, THIS NUDGING inside me, and I can't seem to satisfy it. It's like I belong some-where else, but I don't know where." This is what Tommy admits to our grief group.

I am rendered absolutely mute. That's exactly how I feel.

He gives the group a perplexed look. "I'm starting to do things I've never done before, just trying to figure it all out."

I get that. I totally get that.

"As long as they are healthy things you are trying," the counselor advises.

Healthy things. Right.

"And that's all I want to say tonight," Tommy finishes up.

The rest of the group shares, and I choose not to. I only

halfway listen to them as I play and replay Tommy's words. *There's like this tingling, this nudging inside me, and I can't seem to satisfy it.* It's like he's in my head.

I need to find somebody who completely deserves my justice. Like the Decapitator. Someone who deserves to die.

That will fully salve my core.

"Same time next week," the counselor says, and we all get up.

I follow Tommy out. I'm not the type who strikes up conversations, but with our similar thoughts, I'm want to know about him.

I almost say his name but stop. His blond head is down, like he doesn't want to be bothered. I know that avoidance routine. I respect it.

I dig my keys from my pocket and head to my Jeep, glancing around for the BMW and not seeing it.

"Lane?"

I turn to see Tommy jog across the street to me. Guess I misread his avoidance.

"Hi." His lips twitch and my stomach flutters.

Hmm.

His blue eyes focus in on me. "We went to middle school together. Do you remember me?"

"Yes. You were a year ahead of me."

He nods. "Thought so. Guess I just wanted to say hi and welcome you to the group. I know half the time it's a pain in the ass and the people sometimes drone on, but it'll grow on you."

I nod.

Tommy shoves his hands down inside the front pockets of his jeans and a few awkward seconds pass. I never know what to do in these situations. The other person is obviously waiting for me to say something, but I just don't know what to say.

"You a senior at McLean?" he asks.

"Yes. How about you?"

"Freshman at Mason."

I nod. "I'm planning on going to UVA."

His lips twitch. "Yeah?"

And my stomach flutters again. "Yeah."

"Well." He shrugs. "Guess I'll see you at the next meeting then. Bye."

"Bye." I watch him jog back across the street and my eyes go down to his ass. It's a good ass. Fills out his jeans. He climbs on a motorcycle. Boy's got balls. I'll give him that much. It's thirty-five degrees and he's on a bike. Crazy.

He gives me a two-finger salute as he rolls past, and I nod.

Maybe this grief group won't be so bad after all.

On my way home I drive by Bucky's just to see whatever there might be to see and to watch my rearview for signs of anyone who might be trailing me.

Bucky's place is all lit up, and I catch sight of a woman sitting in a big chair reading. The rest of the windows have curtains, stopping me from seeing inside. I cruise on by, still watching my rearview, but don't see anybody behind me.

I head on home and straight to Justin's room. He's in his jim-jams, lying in bed, reading some graphic novel.

Jim-jams. That's what our mother used to call them.

Justin looks up. "Hi."

I close his door and sit down on his bed. "Tell me everything you know about this Bucky guy."

My brother swallows, and the gurgle of it fills the air between us. He's really nervous.

"I . . . I don't want to," he mumbles.

I take a patient breath. "Why? Are you scared?"

He nods and looks away.

I feel my jaw tighten and concentrate on not looking pissed. I don't want to scare him any more than he already is. "Did he threaten you?"

Justin starts to shake his head, and then he swerves his big hazel eyes over to mine and reluctantly nods. "Please don't tell Dad."

Oh, don't worry about that. I'm taking care of this myself. "What did he do to you?"

"He didn't touch me, just threatened to beat me up if I told anybody. But don't worry, I know how to avoid him."

Anger festers in me. "Where does he hang out?"

"Mostly the trail."

I know exactly what trail Justin's talking about. It weaves through neighborhoods and playgrounds. People use it for biking and jogging. Kids use it to walk home. "How long has this been going on?"

"Only a couple of weeks." Justin fingers his blanket, obviously anxious about the whole subject. "I feel stupid. I thought he was the Masked Savior at first."

"What? Why?"

"Because of the way he was dressed." He rolls his eyes. "Stupid, I know."

"It's not stupid, Justin. Tell me, is he trying to sell you drugs?"

"Yeah. He was giving away some too. You promise you won't tell Dad?"

I concentrate on maintaining a calm expression and not showing the fury boiling through me. Dressing as the Masked Savior and trying to peddle drugs. "You didn't take any, did you?"

"No! I promise! But . . ." He glances away. "Some of the other kids did."

"Justin, stay off that trail. Do you understand me?"

"Yes."

I kiss the top of his head. "Night. See you tomorrow."

As I'm leaving Justin's room, I see Dad in his bedroom looking through photo albums. It reminds me of the two pictures he gave me and that I want to ask him about them.

"Dad?"

With a pleasant smile he glances up, and I find myself smiling back. It's so good to see him happy.

"What's up?" he asks.

"Those two pictures you gave me. One had a dark-haired woman. Do you know who she is?"

He shrugs. "Probably just someone they knew from the marines."

"Were they from Mom's locker at work?"

He heaves a sigh. "No. I still haven't done that yet."

"It's okay." I nod to the photo album. "Well, I'll let you get back to it."

I go to my room, get the picture out, and take another long look at the woman. I don't know . . . I think there's something about this woman my mother didn't want known.

Chapter Twelve

THE NEXT AFTERNOON I USE THE SCHOOL'S
computer to log on to "my" site. I reregister, scroll the posts,
find j_d_l, and see that he is online. My heart kicks in a beat as
I instant message him the same thing I had before:

ARE YOU SURE YOU WANT TO PLAY?

WHO IS THIS? he messages back.

I THINK YOU KNOW WHO . . .

I TRIED TO IM YOU LAST NIGHT BUT IT SAID YOUR ACCT WAS
TAKEN DOWN . . . ??? I THINK YOU'RE MISUNDERSTOOD. I THINK U
NEED A FRIEND.

I resist the urge to roll my eyes. I'm not getting chatty with
this guy. PLAY OR NOT?

He doesn't immediately respond, then: PLAY.

I smile. GOOD. I'LL LEAVE AN ENVELOPE FOR YOU IN THE TRASH IN FRONT OF CVS, CORNER OF HAYCOCK AND RTE 7, FALLS CHURCH. PICK IT UP AT 8 PM. I sign off.

Bucky works at the same CVS. Tonight I'll find out if he and j_d_l are connected. And if the task force just monitored that message, they'll probably be there too. I'll have to be extra cautious, extra alert.

At seven forty-five I'm in my Jeep in the CVS parking lot. There are many stores in this strip mall, many cars, so mine blends in just fine. I don't see any cop cars. Then again if the task force *is* here, they're probably undercover.

I eye the garbage can right in front of CVS. The garbage I've put nothing in. I just want to see who approaches it.

7:50. I get my iPhone ready to snap a few pictures.

7:55. Someone comes out of CVS and someone else goes in.

8:00. An elderly lady throws away a bag of McDonald's.

8:05. A man dressed in a business suit puts his cigarette out in the top tray.

8:10. I glance around the parking lot. What is j_d_l's game? If he was indeed following me the night I did Aisha, I was in Victor's car. If he was following me the night I almost did Jacks, I was in my Jeep. That night I went out to "CVS" a dark car was following me. Then there's the dark BMW that was outside my grief group with a woman behind the wheel. The first dark car could have very well been a BMW. Or maybe the whole thing is just a coincidence.

The thing is—I don't believe in coincidences.

The one thing I do know for certain is that Aisha is now out of the equation because she is in jail.

8:15. A young boy hesitantly approaches the garbage can. He looks around, lifts the lid, and peers inside. He moves things, looks over his shoulder, and then puts the lid back on.

I follow the direction of his look but don't see anything notable. Just cars and people trickling in and out of stores.

The boy walks away in the opposite direction from which he approached, and I fight every urge in me to follow. That boy's a decoy and j_d_l is somewhere watching. I know it.

Sneaky bastard.

He's good at playing my game.

Or maybe that was the task force using a lure.

Either way, I sit right where I'm at, watching cars come and go from the many entrances in and out of the strip mall. Most of them are dark cars. None of them are BMWs.

Bucky emerges from CVS. He doesn't even glance at the garbage can, but he stands for a second and just looks around. His eyes go right over my Jeep before turning away. He walks the length of the shopping center, and I wait until he's all the way down past the grocery store before pulling out.

Several other cars pull out too, all going in different directions.

Slowly I crawl along, keeping track of him as he hangs a right and starts walking along the shadowed sidewalk. The trail my brother mentioned is just a few blocks ahead, and I'd bet anything that's where he's headed.

That trails leads all the way back to the neighborhood where he resides. Which means I'm going to have to park and follow on foot.

In my Jeep I pass him with a glance in the rearview mirror. I don't see one single headlight. No one is following me. I drive beyond the trail's head and park along the street next to a condo building.

As I double-check my supplies, I keep an eye on the sidewalk, waiting for Bucky's appearance.

I survey the area around me again and still see nothing out of the ordinary. Just a dark street and a sprinkling of houses. No one has followed me. I'm certain I'm alone.

Bucky comes up the sidewalk and cuts a right onto the trail.

Silently I climb from my Jeep, and as I follow behind, I lower my mask over my head.

This section of the trail is skinny and bordered by woods on both sides. It's perfect for what I have in store.

Bucky's phone rings, and while he answers, I tune in to my

surroundings one last time. Cold night. The scent of a fireplace in the air. A dog barking way in the distance. Nobody out. Except me and Bucky.

My lips curve. I've got this guy all to myself.

One must control animal instincts, not stimulate them. I don't suppose my aikido sensei would agree with what I'm about to do.

I don't pull my Taser out. I want hand-to-hand with this guy. I need it. "Bucky," I whisper.

He turns.

I go right at it, slamming the heel of my hand into his nose, just like I did Aisha. Blood spurts and I smile.

"What the . . . ?" He stumbles back.

I grab the front of his jacket and knee him in the balls.

He goes down coughing and hacking.

I rear back and kick him in the ribs.

He coughs some more and throws a missed punch in my direction.

I nail him in the eye.

On his butt, he scoots away, blood and saliva driveling from his mouth.

I don't give him a second to retaliate as I whack the blade of my hand into the side of his neck.

He gurgles. "Fuck . . ."

I grab his head and slam it into the ground. "I hate that word."

Bucky holds his hands up. "Stop!"

I look into his eyes. Really look. And see fear there. *That* is the exact look I'm waiting for. I grab a handful of dirt and rub it into his face, and while he spurts, I yank a zip tie around his wrists and take a step back.

Breathing heavily, I look down at his pathetic body and remember him shoving me up against my Jeep. Dickweed. I also remember the first couple of people I took down and the mistakes I made. Look at me now, standing here unharmed. It's too awesome. I raise my Taser.

"Don't!" he screams, and my blood thumps. "God! What do you want? My wallet's in my back pocket."

I lower my voice and ask, "Are you JDL?"

"What? Shit. What the fuck are you talking about?"

"Who did the prostitute and the homeless boy? Who did Jacks?"

"What?" He tries to scoot away again. "I didn't do anything to anybody."

I kneel down and shove the Taser right in his face.

"Wait," he pleads. "What do you want? I'll tell you whatever you want to know."

"Did Aisha do them?"

"Aisha?" He coughs. "She's in jail!"

I know that, you idiot. "What do you know about the Masked Savior?"

He starts to cry. Unbelievable. Not so tough now.

"I've been on the site," he blubbers. "I've posted a few things. But I promise I haven't done anything wrong. I promise."

"Have you been following me?"

"No," he whimpers.

The smell of urine permeates the air, and I don't even glance down to verify he's peed himself. This guy doesn't know anything. He's scared shitless. Or rather, pissless.

"You will stop everything you are doing," I tell him. "Masked Savior website, *drugs* to kids." His eyes widen, and I think of how scared Justin was to tell me about this guy. I grab his throat and squeeze, and he sucks in a raspy breath. "Oh, yeah, I know all about the drugs."

I release him and stand back up. "We clear?"

"Yes! Please, just don't hurt me anymore."

"If I hear your name again, I will find you and I will do so much more." I turn away from him and disappear back down the trail. Sure, I left him zip-tied, but he can still get up and walk home. Or crawl for all I care.

After tonight Justin won't have to be scared again. Because I meant what I said. If I hear Bucky's name one more time, I will do so much more to that asswipe.

When I get back to my Jeep, I stow my mask and drive off. If this guy knew anything about j_d_l, he would've squealed. Bucky's not my copycat. I saw the truth in his face.

Despite what the task force may or may not think, the fact is—as I've already surmised—until another victim shows up, I won't know for sure if Aisha was or was not my impersonator.

As of right now I still think she may have been.

Chapter Thirteen

"THERE'S SOMETHING IN ME THAT NEEDS out," I tell everyone. "It craves release. Sometimes I feel I might explode if I don't give in to it. Yet sometimes I do give in to it, and it's . . . euphoric." *Orgasmic* is what I want to say but figure that's crossing a grief group's line.

Silence reverberates in the already quiet room.

I swallow and sweep my steady gaze over the others. They all look back at me with a mixture of understanding, confusion, and awe.

The counselor steeples his clasped hands. "What a breakthrough you've had, Lane."

I feel it too. It's the first time I've freely spoken in group. Perhaps I'm more comfortable in my thoughts now. Or maybe it's the fact I beat the shit out of Bucky and finally got some relief.

There's more silence, then the counselor trains his gentle eyes on everyone else. "Anyone want to reply to that?"

No one responds. The counselor says a few closing remarks and we are all out the door.

At the Jeep, Tommy strolls over. "Let's get out of here."

I look at his motorcycle. "On that?"

"Yes."

I've never been on a bike. After spilling my guts in grief group, it seems a bike ride might just be a good ending to this evening. Perhaps that's why Tommy invited me. He knows. He can relate.

I stow my Jeep key. "Okay, let's go."

I climb on the back. He offers me a spare helmet and I fit it on. He swings his long leg over the front and revs the engine. It vibrates through my legs, across my stomach, over my breasts, and straight back down to my core.

"Hang on," he throws over his shoulder.

I snake my arms under his leather jacket and around his warm, T-shirt-covered stomach a second before he roars away. I scoot forward a little bit until my front is completely merged with his back. It's cold, but not freezing, as we zip the back roads to Great Falls Park.

We don't stop and just keep going, rolling the hills of

Virginia, up and down and switching right and left. I tilt my head back and gaze up at a clear, star-filled sky. I breathe out a long breath and watch it instantaneously crystallize and then whip away in the wind.

We keep going, and at some point I'm sure we have to be in another state, but we're only in Vienna. I bring my focus back down and look to the right at the sprawling mansions twinkling in the winter darkness. What are the people doing inside those pretty places? Are they happy, content, fighting, grieving . . . ?

We come to a stop, he hangs a left on Chain Bridge, and I realize we're heading back already. I want to ask him to keep going but don't. Hopefully, he'll ask me to do this again. Hopefully.

We go through Tysons Corner and straight back to downtown McLean, where my Jeep is parked.

Tommy pulls up behind my Wrangler and leaves his engine vibrating. I unsnake my arms from his stomach, slowly climb off, and stand for a second while my legs continue to pulse.

Tommy gives me a once-over. "Good?"

I hand him the helmet. "More than good." God, I might just trade my Jeep in for a motorcycle. How stimulating. Freeing. And intoxicating.

"If you ever want to do it again, I hang out mostly at Tysons." With that he drives off.

I watch him leave, filled, oddly enough, with the over-whelming urge to ask him to come back.

I want to do that again.

As I unlock my Jeep, something in my peripheral vision has me glancing up to see a person standing on the other side of the street, about a block down, staring at me. A man or a woman, I can't tell in the nighttime shadows, but just as quickly as the person is there, he or she is gone.

Chapter Fourteen

THAT PERSON IS ALL I CAN THINK ABOUT THE next day. Though I question myself if I really saw someone. I mean, a person doesn't just disappear. Granted there was an alley nearby he or she could've gone down. But it really did seem like they just vanished. My brain has got to be playing tricks on me. People don't just vanish. I walked up and down the street afterward, looking for the phantom person and not seeing him.

I don't know. I just don't know. Could it have been j_d_l?

"Remember that situation I was telling you about?" Kyle asks me, and I glance up from my lunch. "Bucky?" he reminds me.

"Yeah."

"Somebody really roughed him up."

I eat a fry. "You don't say."

Kyle's eyes narrow, just a fraction. "Did you already know that?"

"Nope."

He doesn't immediately respond, then he lowers his voice and says, "I wish I would've been the one to do it."

I've never heard Kyle talk that way before. I take a big gulp of water and wait for whatever he wants to say next.

Instead he takes a step back. "Well, then, see you around."

"Yeah, see you around."

I watch Kyle walk away, feeling for the first time ever something *off* about him.

After school Justin makes sure Daisy is busy on her phone and whispers to me, "Bucky got beat up."

I whisper back, "Mean people deserve that."

His hazel eyes do that wide, innocent thing. "Annie said her brother isn't going to be living with them anymore."

"That's good."

"I told my teacher about the drugs."

I smile at him. "I'm proud of you, Justin. I know that was scary."

"My teacher said Bucky's going to be in a lot of trouble with the police."

"Yes, he will. Especially if you encourage all your friends to speak up too."

"We did."

I shift gears and pull onto Route 7 as Daisy keeps talking on her phone and Justin goes to looking out the window.

"Did the Masked Savior do it?" he asks a couple minutes later.

"I don't know."

"Lane, I think I might be scared of the Masked Savior."

I snap my gaze over to him. "*What?* Why?"

"He used to be cool, but I heard he beat up some people who didn't deserve it. That doesn't sound right to me."

I come to a stop at a red light as guilt nestles itself in. The last thing I would *ever* desire to do is scare my little brother. "Justin, listen to me. You can't believe everything you hear. Rumors are just that. Gossip. Plus, this Savior person only targets bad people and definitely not kids. You're not bad. You shouldn't be scared."

Justin doesn't say anything else and goes back to staring out the window. I shoot him a worried glance, trying to figure out if I should say something but not really knowing what.

We get home a few minutes later, and Victor announces, "Gramps is coming to visit!"

This elicits a grin from Daisy, a hoot from Justin, and a deadpan expression from me. Let's just say Gramps, Victor's father, has never been my favorite. . . .

"Son, I'm telling you. There's just something off with Lane," I overhear Gramps say to Victor.

"*She's fine. She's different, that's all,*" he defends me. . . .

"When's he coming?" I ask.

Victor's face brightens. "Tomorrow!"

My brother and sister explode with enthusiasm.

"For how long?" I ask next.

"A *whole* week!"

This is *so* not what I need right now.

Chapter Fifteen

AT EIGHT O'CLOCK THAT NIGHT I'M IN THE computer room at the public library, staring at the screen, waiting.

"My" site is the only link I have with j_d_l, and he hasn't contacted me since the garbage-can episode.

Thirty minutes ago I sent him a THOUGHT YOU WANTED TO PLAY message that he hasn't bothered to return.

It pisses me off.

Of all the times I need Reggie, it's now. I want to know who's maintaining this site and who the hell j_d_l is. But how would I even explain to Reggie that I want that information? There is no lie I can immediately think of.

I stand up, pace away, stare back at the screen. The lights blink in the library, indicating it's closing.

Well, damn.

I log off and head out and stand in the library parking lot, looking around. I take a deep breath and blow it out, trying to settle myself. But it's in there, deep inside, this anxiousness that needs out.

My brother is scared of the Masked Savior. Which just irritates me all to hell. I want to get out and prowl and figure out this j_d_l and copycat mess but I know the smart thing to do is lay low.

The problem is, I'm not feeling like I want to be smart. Plus . . . Gramps is coming.

I close my eyes and blow out another breath, but it's not working. I need something. *Now.* I imagine this is why people turn to drugs and alcohol. Release. With this thought Zach floats into my mind. . . .

Followed by Tommy. I could use another ride on his bike. That will help with this energy festering in me. Yes, Tommy. I jump in my Jeep and peel out.

If you ever want to do it again, I hang out mostly at Tysons.

Ten minutes later I park at the mall and head inside. I hate it here. The crowds. The crying babies. People packing the walkways with shopping bags. Music blaring out of stores. Way too many smells: perfume, food, herbs.

Yeah, I hate the mall.

But it's where Tommy likely is, so I start walking around, looking in stores, up and down the corridors, and repeat on all the levels.

If only I had his cell number.

Back on floor one I finally give up, buy a cup of coffee, and wander into a bookstore. I round the nonfiction aisle, heading to the pet section, and there he is, sitting in a chair, his blond head ducked as he reads a book on . . . Charles Manson. Huh.

I check out his arm tats again. They're not the typical vine thing most guys wear. They're colorful and patterned. "Hey," I say.

Tommy glances up and pure surprise widens his dark blue eyes. "Well, hey."

"I was looking for you," I honestly tell him.

He closes the book. "Need to get out of here?"

"Yes."

He slips his arms into his black leather jacket. I throw my full coffee away. Without another word we walk out to his motorcycle. He wedges the spare helmet on my head and, holding my gaze, snaps the chin strap. We climb on. My arms find their way under his jacket and around his warm stomach, and I cling as he heads through the night.

I lift my face and stare at the stars, close my eyes and breathe in the cold. I smile and my lips vibrate on a gust of wind. I wonder where he'll take me tonight. Hopefully, like last time, switchbacking on a winding road.

He accelerates onto the interstate, and I duck behind him to hide from the freezing wind. He whips to the right and around a van, then cuts in front and swerves to the left.

Wait, what the hell is he doing?

He picks up speed, flies back to the right, slides into the emergency lane, and zips past a semi.

"Tommy!" I yell, but he doesn't hear me.

Several people honk as he zigzags between the semi and a dump truck, hovers over the yellow dotted line, and peels straight down a row of cars.

My stomach clenches and I squeeze him tighter, hanging on for what feels like my life.

More people honk, a siren pierces the air, and Tommy slices back to the right and off the ramp. He runs a red light, peels into a parking lot and down and around an empty office building. He cuts his engine and waits.

What an asshole.

The cop dashes past, not even seeing us.

Breathing heavily, Tommy finally turns to me. "Was that awesome or what?"

I sniff my frozen nose. "No! No, that *wasn't* awesome. Take me back right now."

His face falls.

What was I thinking? This isn't what I wanted. This isn't what I was looking for. This isn't anything like the other night. This was reckless and stupid. He could've killed us!

Tommy turns around, flicks his engine back on, and slowly, normally, takes me back to Tysons. I don't say a word as I hand him his helmet and charge off.

As I'm unlocking my Jeep, a car cranks, and then revs. The rev is what has me glancing up to see a dark BMW all the way on the other side of the almost empty aboveground garage.

I don't think twice before I take off in a full sprint straight toward it. I want to know who the hell's following me! The car peels out and I keep running. Its tires squeal as it races down the ramp, and I increase my pace, staring at the license plate. I get a partial. A1B. It speeds through the exit, gets honked at, takes a left, and is gone.

I come to a stop, panting, watching it until it disappears from sight.

A1B. At least I have that much. I know now that I didn't imagine the threat of the BMW and the woman driver who is highly probably j_d_l.

Chapter Sixteen

I DON'T NORMALLY SIT IN THE CAFETERIA and look around. I typically read while eating and then head to the library. But today I linger over my taco salad and take the time to watch, to observe. How many of them have been on "my" site?

Over to the right sits Kyle with his other buddies, laughing, talking, seemingly having a grand time.

Straight ahead is Daisy, hanging with a few of her cheerleading friends and a new guy I don't recognize. She's flirting with him, and by the way he's grinning, he loves the attention.

To the left is Zach, with some of his soccer pals and a girl I recognize from the sophomore class. The girl giggles and tosses a fry at him, and he laughs and dodges it.

Maybe that's one of the reasons Zach decided he can't be my friend anymore. Because I don't giggle and toss fries.

Way over near the soft-serve machine is a girl crying. Her friends console her, looking at each other, lost as to what to truly do. A few people in the cafeteria glance their way, then dismiss it. Drama.

I watch her for a minute, puzzling over her freedom of emotion. This is why I'm happy I am who I am. I don't ever want to be that way. That open. That out there. That exposed.

Daisy walks straight toward me, and I snap out of my staring. "Lane, I want you to meet Hammond."

I nod. "Hello, Hammond."

Daisy smiles at him and it's a true smile, not the fake flattery she used to give. "Hammond just moved here from Kentucky. He's a junior."

Hammond shakes my hand. "Daisy's told me a lot about you."

This surprises me.

"All good!" Daisy clarifies as if reading my mind.

"Your sister says everyone calls you Slim?"

"Yes. You can call me Lane if you want."

"Well, anyway"—Daisy nods over her shoulder—"I'll show you where your next class is."

They head off, and I'm not sure why, but my gaze tracks back over to Zach to see him looking at me. He gives me a very tiny acknowledging smile, and I return the gesture. How do I look to him, sitting here alone eating a taco salad and staring at everybody else?

I hope not pathetic.

The bell rings, we all clear out, and I go through the rest of my day. Dark blue BMW. A1B. Reggie could narrow that down for me. But then I'd have to come up with a reason why. *I'm being followed* would freak her out, and the perfect lie is just not coming to me right now.

I'll have to think on it.

When we get home, Gramps has arrived sometime during the day and is already settled in. Daisy and Justin launch themselves at him while Victor watches, laughing. After they all disengage, Gramps turns to me for the obligatory welcome hug. I step up, give it to him, and let go of him just as quickly as he does me.

Just once I'd like him to be as excited to see me as he is my siblings. But that never has happened nor will it probably ever.

We sit through an early dinner of the Daisy and Justin Show while Gramps laughs and talks. I don't say anything. If I do, it'll just earn a grunt from him. I volunteer to clean, mainly because I need something to do.

Victor comes up beside me in the kitchen. "I finally cleared out your mom's personal things from her locker. I'm bringing the box home tomorrow. I want all of us to go through and decide what we do and don't want to keep. Plan on that. Okay? Next I want to do the whole house."

I nod. "Absolutely."

"Dr. Depof recommended it," he rationalizes, like he thinks it might bother me.

It doesn't.

I've already combed through her stuff here, but I definitely want to see what she kept in her office. She was certainly sneaky enough to hide something right within the walls of the FBI, knowing no one would think to look there. Frankly, she would have gotten off on it.

Gramps settles down in front of the TV, simultaneously reading the newspaper, and sometime later says, "Who is this Masked Savior person?"

I bring my head up from the pot I'm scrubbing to see him staring at the TV. The reporter is going on about the local task force, the vigilante acts, if anyone has any information, and on and on.

"Huh," Gramps grunts. "Seems to me this guy is doing everyone a favor around here."

What do you know, maybe ol' Gramps and I have found common ground.

The reporter ends with ". . . and although the chief hasn't specified, an inside source confirms there has been a big break in the case as to the true identity of the Masked Savior."

Big break? Well, damn, what the hell would that be? Clearly, they must not think the Masked Savior and Aisha are one and the same and already behind bars. So what am I missing?

Chapter Seventeen

I WORK MY PATCH AND PAW SHIFT, AND unfortunately "I'm" all anyone can talk about. Masked Savior this and Masked Savior that. It's annoying. When Dr. Issa starts in, I give up, grab Corn Chip, and go outside.

"You okay?" Dr. Issa asks some thirty minutes later.

No, I'm not okay. I've created a monster of a problem with this copycat of mine, and I have no clue how to make it go away.

On top of that there's supposedly a "big break" as to my identity.

Worst-case scenario: The cops somehow know it's me. I just don't see how that's possible, though. I'm always so careful. Plus, they would've arrested me by now.

Best-case scenario: They'll find my copycat, the Masked Savior website will go away, and I can resume my life.

"Lane, you okay?" Dr. Issa repeats.

I nod. "Just thinking about this Savior character. What's your take on it?"

"Good versus evil versus ridiculous."

I turn from Corn Chip to look at him. "Interesting analysis."

"That teen prostitute," he elaborates, "sure she made some bad choices, but did she deserve to be beaten? No. That's the evil side of this guy."

I agree.

"Then there's that rapist and that guy who tortured animals— that's the good side of this guy. They deserved what they got."

I agree. The Weasel and Marco, both done *before* Mom died. "And the ridiculous?"

"Shaving that girl's head. Ridiculous. Seemingly juvenile, if you ask me, and beneath our guy's abilities."

Again, agree. Something I did *after* Mom.

"Either our hero is confused with his game plan, or he has a split personality."

The side door opens, and the receptionist sticks her head out. "Lane, there's a guy here to see you."

That's odd. "Okay." I toss the ball back to Corn Chip, don't look at Dr. Issa, and head straight out to the parking lot to find

Tommy standing next to his bike holding his helmet. My stomach muscles twitch.

He doesn't smile. "Hey."

"How did you know I work here?"

"I ride by here a lot on my way to school. I caught sight of your Jeep and decided to stop."

I wait for whatever it is he wants.

"I'm sorry about the other night. I get crazy sometimes. Ever since my sister died, I've been lost, looking for something, anything to make me feel again. Sometimes I find it, but then it's gone. I know what I did was stupid. Hell, I knew it as I was doing it, but I can't seem to stop. The adrenaline. The pumping blood. At least it makes me feel alive. If even for a few seconds." He lays his hand over his heart and rubs it. "There's this huge emptiness in me and I want to fill it, but I don't know how." He stops, takes a breath. "Anyway, there it is. That's got to be the most I've said to anyone in a very long time."

I don't immediately respond to his words that make too much sense. I take in his wind-messed blond hair and honest, yet lost and confused eyes. And then I decide to be just as honest. "For me it's darkness. It's an itch I need desperately scratched. It's a craving that once satisfied keeps coming back."

He nods, and I find myself perplexed by the fact I just told him all that. Yet it feels so good that I did.

"Maybe you and I need to try some adrenaline sports," he suggests. "Bungee. Parachuting. Shark diving."

Actually, that doesn't sound like too bad of an idea. "I went to church," I tell him, as long as we're sharing. "Found some clarity."

"Church." He mulls that around. "Haven't tried that yet."

"Maybe we'll go sometime."

"Yeah, maybe." Tommy takes a tentative step toward me. "So can we try again? At being healing friends?"

Healing friends. I kind of like that choice of words.

"Yes," I say, even though I know deep down I'll never heal. I'll always be who I am.

Tommy gives me a hug that at first starts out awkward and slowly turns into being okay. He smells like leather. Zach always smells like boy-scented body wash. Why am I comparing their smells?

Tommy brushes a kiss across my cheek and steps back.

My insides do the fluttery girlie thing, and I frown. *Fluttery girlie thing?* That's not me. But I *liked* that kiss. He has whiskers, and they feel good. *Real* good.

Then why am I frowning? If I like something, shouldn't I be smiling? Yes, but I don't want to be fluttery and girlie. I want to be focused.

He doesn't look at me as he rumbles off on his bike. After he's gone, I turn to head back into Patch and Paw and catch Dr. Issa still standing in the side yard, watching us through the fence.

He quickly turns away, trying to make it look like he wasn't staring, and I find this oddly amusing. So Dr. Issa is snooping about me and biker guy. Isn't that something?

When I get home, Daisy and Hammond are sitting on our front steps, holding hands and talking. He sees me getting out of my Jeep, gives Daisy a good-bye kiss on the cheek, sends me a wave, and walks off.

Daisy sits there, watching him, and when I finally reach her, she glances up. "I've got it bad."

This is where I normally brush her off, but with us being more sisterly now, I take a seat. "Yeah?"

Her face curves into a dreamy smile. "Yeah," she chuckles. "He doesn't believe in sex before marriage. He doesn't drink or do drugs. I mean, where'd this guy come from, right?"

"That sounds great." So different from what she's ever done before.

She looks at me, like she's completely perplexed with her own self. "Yeah, it really does."

We share a smile, and the front door opens. Victor takes a second to look between us, like he can't believe his daughters are having a "moment."

"Ready for our help?" Daisy asks, then turns to me. "We're clearing out some of Mom's stuff for storage."

"Yeah, Dad told me." I can't wait.

He tosses me a key. "That's to our file cabinet. The whole bottom drawer is full of stuff she threw in there. Just put it all in the box I brought from work and leave it in the office. I'm going to go through it tonight."

I already picked the lock on the filing cabinet. I know what's in there. Nothing really.

He turns to Daisy. "You hit the bathroom and clear out all her makeup and products. Both you girls go through her jewelry and clothes and see if you want anything. I'll be in the basement with Gramps." With that he walks off.

Daisy looks at me. "This is morbid."

"I know." I give her an understanding smile. "But it has to be done. Why don't you wait for me, and I'll help you do their bedroom."

"It's okay," she reassures me. "I'll get started."

"Hey." I stop her as she's getting up. Three months ago she would've never been this mature. I'm proud of her. "I like being your sister," I tell her.

Playfully she rolls her eyes. "Don't go getting all mushy on me, Lane."

I laugh with her and we head inside. I go straight to the office and look around. In the corner of the room sits a box I assume is the one Victor brought home from work. I lift the lid.

Inside are things you'd find on a person's desk. Stapler. Hole punch. Family picture. Along the side are several files. I glance at their tabs: TRANSCRIPTS, INSURANCE, PERSONAL.

I thumb through the transcripts and insurance ones, don't see anything of interest, and then slide the personal one out. I give the hallway a quick glance, see it empty, and open the file.

Right on top sits a stack of old report cards with straight As. Not surprising.

Next are a bunch of drawings, and according to the initials and date in the corner, Mom did them when she was a teenager. Drawings of people I assume must have been her high school friends. I never knew she got into artsy stuff. One catches my eye and I slip it out.

It's of a dark-haired girl, and something about her seems very familiar. I study it for a second, thinking, and then it occurs to me . . . the two pictures Victor gave me of Seth and Mom. There was a dark-haired woman, and, yes, her hair, her eyes, her long face—they're one and the same. The drawing's just a younger version of her.

Whoever she is, my mom knew her when they were teenagers.

I keep that drawing out and continue going through the rest of the file. There are newspaper clippings announcing her achievements throughout the years: childhood, teenage, and older. Clippings of her making the honor roll or later with her FBI cases.

I riffle through the rest, and at the very back of the file, taped to the inside, is a small yellow envelope. I peel it off, open the flap, and shake the contents into my palm.

A key. With no tag. The numbers 963 are engraved on the square head.

I hold the key up and study it. It doesn't look like any of the keys to this house. Or to any of the filing cabinets in here. Maybe it's to something at FBI headquarters.

Or perhaps 4 Buchold Place. Or that house in Maryland where she held Zach.

I rotate the key, giving it a good solid study. But the more I stare at it, the more I convince myself whatever it unlocks is not going to be good.

Victor and Gramps come up from the basement, and I quickly fold the drawing and slide it and the key into my pocket. I go back to what I'm supposed to be doing and unload the bottom drawer of the filing cabinet. I wedge the lid on the box and set it on the desk for Victor to go through tonight like he said.

When I come out of the office, Victor and Gramps are talking in the kitchen. I give them both a little smile and head straight up to the master bedroom to find Daisy sitting on their bed, staring at a card.

"What's that?" I ask.

"An old birthday card of mine I found in Mom's stuff."

I sit down beside her. "You okay?"

"Actually, I just had this really strange memory." She waves the card in the air. "It happened on my eighth birthday."

"What's the memory?"

"Mom and Dad were arguing. Here in their bedroom. The door was closed. I stopped to listen. Probably because I never really heard them go at it before."

"What were they arguing about?"

Daisy's brows come together. "Marji, I think. Do you know that name?"

Chapter Eighteen

I ASSURED DAISY SHE WAS PROBABLY MIS-remembering, and she reluctantly dropped the whole thing. Marji. The woman from Richmond. When we got that card in the mail, Victor said he didn't know a Marji. Either he's lying or he didn't remember.

Whichever it is, I'm going to find out. Mom did nothing but lie to me. I'm not going to get caught up in that with Victor. When the time is right, I'll ask him.

I put that aside for now and focus on the mystery key. I scan it and spend an hour researching what it might go to. But I get nothing. Then I do some searches combining Marji's name and my mom's and then Marji and Richmond. But likely Marji's short for something, and I don't know her last name, so

I basically get nowhere on that as well. Also I type *blue BMW* with partial plate A1B, and nothing comes back. Not that I thought it would. Maybe I should go into law enforcement, or computers, like Reggie. It'd sure make things easier on my end.

As I go to sleep, my thoughts switch to this "big break" the news reported, and I wonder if Catalina's task-force father has shared this information with Victor. Then I begin to think of Catalina and how I might be able to use her to my advantage.

The next morning I go downstairs to see Victor frying bacon, slow and on low heat like Mom used to do. His expression seems distant, and I imagine he's remembering her too.

"You don't have to do that just because Mom did," I softly tell him.

He glances up, and although he's masking it, I see the sorrow deep in his eyes. "It's important to keep ritual going."

No, it's not, I want to say, but nod my head. I double-check the living room to make sure we're alone and then tell him about Daisy's memory and more importantly Marji. "We got a condolence card from a Marji." I'm careful not to accuse him of lying. "Could they be one and the same?"

He doesn't look at me and instead just stares at the bacon, and I get the impression he's trying to figure out how much to tell me. "Yes. I'm sorry I wasn't honest with the facts. She's a longtime friend of your mom's. I . . ." He glances over at me.

"Let's just put it this way. I respected your mom's relationship with her because they were childhood friends. But I didn't care for her. I didn't want her around the house or you kids."

Whoa. Okay.

"Let's just leave it there," he tells me. "All right?"

I nod, he goes back to the bacon, and my brain whirls with what he just said. Mom had a childhood friend, Marji, who lives in Richmond, and Victor didn't like her. I want to ask him why but know he won't say any more.

"Mind helping?" he asks. "Mix the pancake batter for me?"

"Sure." I go about getting out the bowl, ingredients, and whisk, and my brain tracks back to those two pictures he gave me. One had a dark-haired woman in it. I bet that's Marji. But if he didn't like her, why give me that picture? I know he wants to drop the subject, but I ask anyway.

He lets out a patient breath. "Yes, the third person is Marji. I wanted you to have pictures of your real father and mom. That's all. I honestly didn't think the subject of Marji would ever come up in this household. Other than that condolence card, we haven't heard from her in years."

"Okay." I accept it and drop the subject. I can tell he's getting irritated. He would get even more irritated if he found out Marji sent me a card as well.

A few quiet minutes go by filled only by the sizzling of bacon and the soft voices of the news filtering in from the living room. I scoot in beside Victor, pour pancake mix on the flat griddle, and watch it slowly bubble. He slides the cooked bacon out and lays new pieces down.

"Your army friend with the daughter," I start. "Catalina?"

"Yeah?"

"Where does she go to school?"

"Homeschooled. Why?"

I'd preplanned my response and answer easily, "She and I hit it off a little, and I thought I might see if she wants to hang out."

And I thought I might use her for information.

This surprises Victor in a hooray-my-daughter's-normal way. "Wow, um, okay."

I hate that I've made him happy with a lie.

"I'll give you their number, and you can take things from there."

"Thanks." That's all we say about Catalina and my upcoming planned snooping of her dad.

After breakfast I dial her number. "This is Lane, we met the other day."

"Yeah, hey," she responds, as if she'd been expecting my call.

I find this oddly comforting. "Thought we might hang out sometime." I like to get right to the point.

"Okay. My place or yours?"

Sounds more like a proposition. "Yours."

"Today?"

I like this girl. "Yes."

"One o'clock. My address is . . ."

I jot it down, say bye, and sit for a second puzzling her. Seems as if she likes to get right to the point as well.

At one I ring her doorbell.

She swings the door open. "So," she says and plants her hand on her hip, "what's your story?"

I look at her skinny jeans, tight tee, and Pumas and almost laugh. I'm skinny. She's skinny. I'm tall. She's tall. I have red hair. She has curly black hair. I'm fair. She's olive.

She's like the dark mirror image of me.

I glance past her into the house—it appears empty—and then I bring my gaze back to hers. "My story?" I ask.

"No one's home." She answers my look. "You're either here (a) for my hot older brother, (b) to see what it's like to be with a lesbian, or (c) you want my dad to get you out of a ticket. So which is it?"

This girl's going to see right through my bullshit, and so I proceed. "One, the hot older brother is more my sister's thing; two, I'm not a lesbian but that's cool if you are; and three, I don't have any tickets. *But* I am here because of your dad."

This causes her dark brows to lift. "What can my detective father do for you?"

I improvise on the spot. "He's on the Masked Savior local task force. I registered on the site. Then I took my registration down. Basically, I want to make sure my ass isn't going to get busted. *And* I heard there's a 'big break' in the case and, frankly, I'm probing what that is."

Catalina's mouth curves into a huge grin. "Lane, my tall, skinny new friend, we're going to be good pals." She motions me inside her house. "You've just met the moderator of Masked Savior dot com."

My heart skips an excited beat. Well, holy damn, this chick may very well know the true identity of j_d_l.

"Although I don't know what that 'big break' is," she continues, "I'm more than willing to snoop and find out."

I'm more than willing to help her snoop. Catalina, my curious new alliance.

"So what do you think of the site?" she asks.

I shrug. "Some people seem kind of stupid. Others seem like they're really into the vigilante thing."

She rolls her eyes. "Did you see that one guy that posted a brownie recipe?"

No, I didn't, but I fake a laugh as I follow her up to her room. "I know. How stupid. Since you're the moderator, you probably have everyone's real names." *Like j_d_l.* "You should make that brownie recipe and send it to the guy," I stupidly joke.

She laughs but doesn't confirm one way or another if she

has the real identities of people. I don't press it any further. I'll differ my tactic next time I'm with her.

She walks down a wood-planked hall and through an open door into her bedroom. I give it a quick glance. Purple walls. Black comforter. Silver metal desk. Messy. Disorganized. Not my kind of room.

Catalina plops down across her bed, leaving me to decide where to sit. I grab a wad of clothes off her desk chair, lay them aside, and take a seat.

"What are your thoughts on this Aisha person? Do you think she's the real Masked Savior or not?" she asks.

I shrug. "Well, another victim hasn't popped up since she's been in jail, so despite what the task force says, she may very well be."

Excitement glints across her eyes. "I thought the same thing. But then that guy got beat up on the trail. . . . What was his name?"

Bucky.

She waves that question off. "You don't think that's connected somehow?"

"Nah, not really the style."

She leans forward. "Know what I think? I think there's more than one person involved with all this."

"Really?"

She narrows her eyes. "Taser. Zip ties. Baseball bat. Turning some people in to the cops, and others not. It's almost like there's the real vigilante, and then there's someone else who *thinks* they are a vigilante."

Catalina *is* a smart one.

She grins. "It's all very mysterious."

"Yes. It is." Why didn't I think to connect with Catalina sooner?

Chapter Nineteen

THE NEXT NIGHT I PARK MYSELF IN FRONT of my laptop and scroll through "my" site. One username catches my attention, and I pause.

[KyleScienceGuy] Getting bored. When's the next M.S. victim?

Kyle, as in the guy from school. Kyle, who I have known forever. He's an active member on "my" site. I don't like this at all.

I continue moving through the pages of posts but don't see any more from j_d_l. Now that I know Catalina is the administrator, I study several of the usernames. None seem like her, though.

My phone rings and I check the display. Catalina. "Hey."

"Hey," she says. "I did some snooping. I don't know exactly why, but the cops are positive Aisha has nothing to do with the

Masked Savior. They do, however, have solid evidence that the Masked Savior is . . ."

I take a breath and hold it.

". . . a female. And young."

My brain spins about a million miles out of control. "But *Aisha* is female and young."

"I know, but for whatever reason they know for sure she's not involved. You ready for the best part?"

A tingle runs through my body. "I'm ready."

"Remember how we were talking that we think there's a real vigilante and then someone else who is copycatting?"

Copycatting. She's using my word. "Yes."

"This is super secret. . . ."

"I won't say anything," I assure her.

"The cops think the same thing. *But* they're not officially releasing that. That's majorly under wraps."

"So the cops think there are two, and they think female and young. Do they believe the real Savior and the copycat are *both* female and young?"

"No," she says. "They think one is female and one is male."

How would the cops know this? My copycat aside, *I'm* always so careful. The way I dress is masculine. When I speak I disguise my voice. My movements are certainly not feminine.

Unless the people I've targeted or the evidence I do leave

somehow points the investigators to female and young. Or maybe they think the real Masked Savior is male and the copycat is female.

"You said you were sort of on the fence about Aisha. What do you think now?" I ask.

"I've officially changed my mind. I think they're right about her being innocent. I think the real Masked Savior is out there, and I think the copycat is live and active on the website."

Me too. Hearing Catalina voice my thoughts validates my hypothesis. Either way, the cops really do have a big break. Proving I now more than ever need to stay low in my search for j_d_l, who I know followed me and who I now *highly* suspect is also my copycat.

"Oh, and I have a question," she says. "I looked for your registration on the site but didn't find it."

"I registered under a fake name." I also took it down.

She laughs. "Oh, Lane. I like you more and more each time we talk."

Truth is, I feel the same way.

Kyle comes up to me the next day after school. "I heard you and Catalina know each other."

"Yes. How do you know her?"

"I tutor her in physics."

They know each other. They've talked about me. Kyle's on "my" site. Catalina's the site administrator. They're both Masked Savior fans, and they both now think I am too.

"She mentioned you guys talked about the Masked Savior," he says.

"We did." How well do they know each other? Did she tell him about her snooping and the information she uncovered?

"So . . . you want to go get dinner or something later?" he asks.

I fight the overwhelming urge to hit him upside the head. *Really? Now we're soul mates or something because we all have talked about the Savior?* But this isn't polite conversation and so I reply instead, "Busy. Work. See ya later."

He nods, all cool, even though he's not. "See you later, then."

I meet Daisy at my Jeep, and we head over to the elementary campus to pick up Justin. The kiss-and-ride line is longer than usual, and we take our spot to wait. Daisy gives her customary impatient breath and pulls out her phone to check messages.

True, most people hate waiting, but it's never bothered me. I see waiting as an opportunity to think. To look around. To observe others when they don't know someone's watching.

Like the guy behind me picking his nose.

Or the woman across the street chewing gum.

"Look at that." Daisy nods over to the right where a pack of elementary boys are coming down the sidewalk dressed as the Masked Savior.

Inwardly I sigh. Without meaning to, I really have developed a fan club. This all desperately needs to go away.

"I am so sick of this superhero thing," Daisy says.

With this I totally agree. Frankly, I never understood the concept of Superman or Spiderman. Perhaps people have some need to hand their problems over to a larger-than-life character.

I, however, am not one of those people. I prefer to handle my own shit.

Justin finally emerges. He hops in the back and we head home.

Gramps has made us a snack, and while Justin and Daisy dig in, I head up to my room. Five minutes later Gramps knocks, and I glance up to see him hovering in my doorway.

I give him a fake smile. "Hi, Gramps."

He doesn't smile back. "Your stepdad says you've been gone a lot at night."

Gramps always refers to his son as my stepdad when everyone else I know calls him Victor or my dad. "Yes."

"Where do you go?"

"The coffee house to study."

"Which coffee house?"

My inner alarm goes off. "Down the road."

"Hmm."

I decide not to say anything else and wait for whatever he wants.

"I don't know what you do at night, but I don't think you go study. You've got your stepdad fooled. I think you're up to no good."

I get really still. He didn't follow me last night, did he? "Why do you think I'm up to no good?"

He doesn't answer and instead looks around my room. "I'm a retired principal, and I raised five kids. I'm not stupid."

No, I never said he was stupid. But he's definitely annoying.

Gramps brings his eyes back to mine. "Why do you have journals about serial killers in your closet?"

Anger sparks in me. He's seen my collection of news clippings, personal research, notes. "Why did you go in my closet?"

"Answer me."

"Mom and Dad both work with serial killers. I started researching them too. What's the big deal?"

"Does your stepdad know?"

Mom had accidentally found the box months ago. Her concern surrounding it is laughable now. "Mom knew and I'm pretty sure she told him." Though I doubt she did. "I'll show him tonight if you want me to." There, maybe that'll throw Gramps off. "I'm not hiding anything."

Gramps rolls his eyes over to the closet. He doesn't say anything else, just turns and is gone.

I swallow my suddenly dry throat and immediately get up. I grab my box from the top shelf of the closet, slide open my underwear drawer, and tuck it among all the cotton undies. It's the only place I can think that somebody won't go prying again.

Chapter Twenty

THERE'S A NEW GIRL IN GROUP THERAPY, AND she's droning on and on about her sorrowful self. Beside me sits Tommy, and I can tell he's bored as well. Five minutes in I catch him totally zoned out and figure that's my green light to do the same. I tune the girl out and allow my thoughts to drift as I indulge my fantasies. . . .

I crouch in the darkness, my breathing steady and calm, my pulse fluttering in anticipation. The deviant I'm following knows I'm here, and his own breathing quickens as his pounding heart echoes in the night around us. I stand to my full height and step from the shadows to see his eyes widen in realization that I'm here for him. I take my Taser out, raise it, and—

Tommy nudges me. "Lane," he whispers.

I blink, glance around the group, and see every eye focused on me. "Yes?"

"It needs to be unanimous," the counselor says. "We all know we've lost a loved one, but we've yet to share *how* we lost that loved one. It needs to be unanimous," he repeats. "Everyone's agreed to share but you."

"Oh." I glance over to Tommy. Why I glance at him, I'm not entirely sure. "Okay." *Mine was murdered.* This is what I'll say and spare the details.

The girl a few seats to my left starts. She lost her mom to breast cancer. The guy beside her lost his twin brother in a swimming accident. Guy beside him lost his grandfather to a heart attack. And on around the circle it goes.

When it's Tommy's turn, he quietly starts, "My sister was a preschool teacher. She was the Decapitator's last victim."

I sit up in my chair. *What?*

He continues, "Well, that's not true. The last victim was an FBI woman." Then that's all he says.

I know it's my turn, but all I seem able to do is replay his words:

She was the Decapitator's last victim.

Tommy gives me another nudge, indicating I need to go.

I turn and look him straight in the eyes. "My mother was that FBI woman."

Everyone in the room gasps. So much for me sparing details.

The counselor finishes out the meeting, and although I don't look at Tommy again, I *know* he's staring at me. I imagine he wants to get out of here as much as I do. The counselor dismisses us and I beeline for my Jeep.

He had to have known who I am. Everyone at school knows who my mom was and how she died. Then again, he doesn't go to my school. But it was heavily covered by the media. How could he not know who I am?

My sister was a preschool teacher. She was the Decapitator's last victim. Her hands and feet were delivered in a cooler. I watched the video of her death. A video my mother sent me.

My parents killed his sister. They cut her into pieces. They enjoyed it. Oh my God. I've got to get out of here.

"Lane?" Tommy stops me.

I spin and look him square in his confused eyes. "How could you not tell me?"

He takes a tiny step back. "That means you're the niece of the Decapitator. Your uncle murdered my sister."

As the story goes. "How could you not tell me?" I repeat.

"And also murdered your mother," he continues, obviously working things through in his mind. "I didn't know. After my sister died, I couldn't take it. It was killing me. I ended up leaving and staying with some family in New York. I knew there was an FBI woman, but I didn't know she was your mother."

I don't know what to do, what to say, and so I just stare

into his perplexed eyes and . . . I honestly don't know if I believe him.

Tommy blows out a breath and runs his fingers through his blond hair. "I need to go. I need to think through all this."

That's probably a good idea.

On a second thought, he turns back. "Just when I think I'm getting better . . ."

Getting better. I never thought of myself as getting better, as something needing to be cured. I am who I am. I only need to perfect the details of dealing with that.

"Are you *blaming* me?" I ask. Because it sure sounds like he is.

Tommy shakes his head. "Your uncle violently murdered my sister. It's a lot to take in." He swings his leg over his bike, gives it a crank, and is gone.

It *is* a lot to take in. I thought I'd found a new friend in Tommy, but I'm not entirely sure we can be friends with this between us now. If the situation was reversed, if his uncle killed my sister, I probably wouldn't want anything to do with him either.

Chapter Twenty-One

ALL THE WAY HOME I THINK ABOUT TOMMY, j_d_l, Marji, and where all this started—with my mother— which circles my brain around to the mysterious key that I have yet to identify.

I need Reggie's help. As soon as I get to my room I pull up the scanned image, send it to her, and then call her.

"We found this key. . . ." I begin weaving my tale when she answers her phone. "It was in Mom's personal stuff. We can't figure out what it goes to. Victor said he's really busy at work and will look into it in a few months. I thought you might be able to help get us there sooner."

She doesn't say anything.

"Reg?"

She sighs. "This is it, Lane. I'll help you with this and then no more. We used to talk about stuff. We used to be *real* friends. But lately all it is with you—if I hear from you at all—is what I can do to help you research something."

I don't respond. Neither does she. Seconds tick by, and with each one guilt nestles in. She's right. I didn't even bother to say hi. Or ask about MIT. Or see how she's holding up after Mom. I'm a horrible friend.

"I'm sorry," I tell her.

"Thanks for apologizing, but I mean it. This is it."

I've never heard her voice so resolute. I've really pissed her off. Other than apologizing, which I just did, I don't know what to do.

"I'll look into the key and send you what I find. Talk to you later." With that she clicks off.

I sit and just stare at my phone. I can't lose Reggie. She's been my only real friend. What can I do? The only thing is to give it some time and then call her and have a real conversation with her, like we used to.

I go downstairs, and Gramps is in the kitchen prepping the crock pot for tomorrow. This is his last night with us. I try not to show my joy over this wonderful fact as I go to the refrigerator and grab a Coke.

"Coke?" he comments. "You should be drinking milk."

Milk? What am I, five? But I take a patient breath, put the Coke back, and grab the milk.

"I have good news," he announces.

Daisy and Justin turn from the TV, and I hope it's something along the lines of *I won the lotto and am heading on a world tour!*

"I've talked to your dad and decided to stay on a little longer than I initially thought."

Disappointment creeps through my body, but I concentrate extremely hard on curving at least part of my lips into what I hope might pass as a pleased smile.

Justin jumps for joy. "How long?"

Gramps grins. "Thinking a month."

A month!

Daisy squeals and launches herself across the living room into Gramps's arms. Justin does the happy dance. I put the milk back, grab that Coke, and head straight up to my room.

Maybe I can move into our tree house. . . . I close my eyes. A month. Okay, I can do this. Just act normal, come and go, interact with him the least amount possible, and keep as low a profile as I can.

I'm in my bedroom the next afternoon, and my phone rings. I check the display. Reggie. I blow out a breath. "Hey."

"The key is to a locker at the Dunn Loring Metro station."

No niceties. Just to the point. She really is pissed. "Thank you, Reg. I'll tell Victor."

"Why would your mom have a locker at a Metro station?"

The lie comes easily. "She sometimes took that train into DC." A few seconds go by. I'm not sure how to apologize again, but I have to try. "Reg . . ."

"Listen, I've got to go. I'll talk to you later." She hangs up, and something deep inside me stitches with sorrow.

She's not ready to hear my apologies. She's not ready to have a friendly conversation. I get that and I have to respect it. I'll call her next week. Surely, she'll be ready to talk by then.

I slip my coat on, ignore Gramps's disapproving glare, and drive straight over to the Dunn Loring station.

It's packed with people just getting off work and in from DC. I find a parking spot all the way in the back and hike it through the freezing cold to the entrance.

As I join the crowd coming and going, I make my way into the dim interior. I have no clue where the lockers are, spend a few minutes looking around, ride the escalator down and then back up, and finally locate them in a corner of the upper floor.

Pulling the key from my pocket, I find 963 in the bottom left, and pause . . . suddenly not so sure anymore.

What am I going to find? Why have a locker if not to conceal something really bad? Why not just have a safety-deposit box?

Because—I imagine—safety-deposit boxes have to have

another name listed in case something like this happens. A death.

Or maybe all that's in this locker is something she didn't want to take on the Metro with her, like a bag, and I'm totally overreacting.

Okay. I nod. *Here goes.*

Crouching down, I fit the key in and turn the lock. A small hinged door pops open, and inside sits a box. I slide it out, dying to open it, but knowing I should wait until I'm somewhere private.

I close and lock the door, turn, and immediately sense someone watching me. I stand, looking around the dim interior, scanning faces, searching corners, studying what people carry with them.

Still prickling with awareness, I make my way through the crowded tunnel. As I step outside, I pause to glance one last time over my shoulder and catch someone ducking behind a farecard machine.

The guy behind me smacks right into me. "Stupid tourist," he mutters.

I resist the overwhelming urge to jab my fingers in his eyeballs, and continue moving with the crowd. When I'm free from the horde, I find a place near the bus stop and take a seat on one of the benches in plain sight of the Metro exit.

I stay for an hour, dying to look in the box, but definitely more interested to see if someone is following me. I make eye contact with every face, searching for a hint of recognition and coming up with nothing. I'll sit here the whole frigid night if I have to. That person can't stay in there forever. Unless . . . he or she hopped a train to another station.

That thought is what finally has me standing up and heading to my Jeep.

My cell buzzes. It's Victor. COMING HOME FOR DINNER?

YES, I type back. If anything to keep Gramps off my ass. I'LL BE THERE IN 20.

Enough time for me to quickly look in the box. I climb in my Jeep, peel the tape off the cardboard, open the flaps, and reach inside.

Chapter Twenty-Two

THE FIRST PICTURE IS OF MY MOM, VERY pregnant, and my real dad with his hand on her belly. We look like a normal happy little family. Yet we were anything but. A pang of something I can't quite identify echoes through me. Loss for the happiness we never had. Sorrow for the nightmare they were. Anger over the deceit of it all.

The second picture is of my mom, my real dad, and that same dark-haired lady, who I now know is Marji. They're sitting in a bar, toasting with beer mugs. I study her face for a second and think of the drawing I have of her.

The next several pictures are of my mom and my real dad having . . . sex. My lip curls in disgust as I look at their naked, intertwined bodies. Who took these pictures?

All the rest are of their kills. All those women. Preschool teachers, just like Tommy's sister. Innocent. Young.

Bile swells in my throat as I take in my real dad, grinning over a gruesome corpse. Of my mom in action sawing off a hand. And of Marji laughing as she watches. I tear my gaze away, suddenly unable to breathe. Holy God. Marji was part of their killing orgy.

I purposefully don't look at the other pictures and instead reach for the manila envelope at the bottom. I open it and peek inside to see a stack of stationery notes. They're in a variety of colors: yellow, blue, pink. . . . I pull one out, noting my hands are shaking, and study the slanted penmanship for a second before I read:

Suzie, I wish you could've seen what Lane and I did to my neighbor's cat today. Only you can appreciate it. I miss you. I love you. ~Marji

I open my Jeep door, stumble out, and throw up.

Suzie, my mom's name. And Marji. Oh my God, what did I do to that cat?

"Hey, are you okay?"

I wipe my mouth and glance over my shoulder at an elderly lady standing a cautious distance away. "Yes, ma'am. I'm on my way home."

She nods and heads off.

I take a few needed seconds to steady myself.

When I'm ready, I get back in my Jeep and dump out the rest of the contents. A mixture of stationery notes and the matching envelopes they originally came in. I note the return address in Richmond and her real name: Marjoream Vega. I look at the postmark and quickly calculate it as fifteen years ago. I would've been two. One year before I witnessed the first decapitation. Had this Marji woman been there for that, too?

More important, is she still at this Richmond address?

I make myself look through the other notes. All from Marji to Suzie.

> . . . I saw Junior today.
> Remember him? Ha-ha! . . .

> . . . I bought that property I was
> telling you about . . .

> . . . Too bad Victor's such a dick . . .

On they go. Tons of cards with random thoughts in the same slanted writing. I don't even try to make sense of them.

I put all that aside and look back in the box, where one last envelope sits. This one is white and blue and looks official.

Flipping it over, I note the medical-lab stamp. I open it and slip out a thin sheet of paper. PATERNITY TEST is listed in the top right corner, and I quickly scan the random fields. The last line at the bottom jumps out at me, and I catch my breath.

TEST SUBJECT: Daisy Cameron
PATERNAL RESULTS: Seth Leaf

I drive home in a numb haze. I sit through dinner, but I can barely eat. Daisy is my *real* sister. According to the date stamp on the test results, Mom always knew. I don't get it. Why marry Victor? My gaze trails to him. Does he know? Surely not. I can't imagine he would've stayed with Mom if he knew me and Daisy were both Seth's daughters.

Across my uneaten meatloaf, Daisy catches my eye. *Everything okay?* she mouths, and I nod. She has their evil blood running in her, too. Wait. Did they ever do anything to her, make her participate, make her watch like they did me? *Train* her?

Nausea waves through me, and my throat closes together. Oh, God no. Please no.

"Lane?"

I glance over at Victor. "I don't feel well," I say, and run for the downstairs bathroom, where I lose what little I have left in my stomach.

Daisy. She's so opposite from me. Outgoing to my not.

Happy to my stoic. At least now she is. Before Mom died, she was so mean. Always poking at me. Lying at school. Manipulating her friends and boys. Is that all, though? Does she keep secrets like I do? Does she have another life that none of us know about?

I groan. Not Daisy. Not my little sister.

Victor pushes the bathroom door open. "Sweetheart, are you sick? What's wrong?"

I take the ginger ale he's holding out and gulp some down. "I think I ate something bad at lunch. I threw up earlier, too."

"Go on upstairs and get in bed. I'll bring you some toast later."

"Okay." As I pass by the dining room, I give my family a small smile. Daisy is all I think about the rest of the night. I pick through every memory, analyzing them, looking for similarities in me.

What I come up with is that Daisy used to have this dark side to her, but it was all on the outside, whereas mine stays inside and secretive. I want to talk to her, but I don't want to set off any alarm bells. So I'll watch. Carefully watch. I'll steer her in the correct path. The path *I* have not chosen, but I'll make sure she does.

During my library TA job I look her up. Marjoream Vega from Richmond, Virginia. Sure enough, she's still at the same address. I don't write it down. I know it by heart. I *will* be paying her a visit.

She's the last link to the decapitations. If I have to kill her, I will. I have no qualms about that. But I need to know exactly how she was involved.

I do my Patch and Paw shift after school, and when it's over I go straight to the cremation room. I have to protect my family. I crank the gas flames, open the door, and toss the box from the locker inside. *This is big enough to put a body in.* That thought floats through my mind and surprises me. I give the furnace another look. Yes, it is big enough for a human body. If I ever need it.

I tuck that away for later and focus back on the box and my (and Daisy's) disturbing legacy.

"What are you burning?" Dr. Issa asks.

"Stuff I want to forget," I honestly tell him.

Through the fireproof glass I watch the pictures melt into a sick puddle. It was all a game to the three of them. Some twisted, horrible game.

"You okay?" he quietly asks.

His question. His tender voice causes tears to unexpectedly press my eyes. But I don't turn and let him see them. Instead I just nod my head.

A few quiet seconds pass and I hear him click the door, shutting us in the tiny room. "As you already know," he begins,

"Zach and I lost our mom several years back. I used to hide in plain sight. Tell everyone I was okay. Frankly, if one more person asked me how I was doing, I thought I might hurt them. I know this is peculiar, but I used to carry around a lock of my mom's black hair. It's what I remember most about her. All that hair. Zach turned to alcohol to deal, and I did things I'm not proud of."

I turn away from the dying flames and bring my wet eyes up to his. "Like what?"

He takes a step closer, putting us just a few inches apart. "I yelled at my dad for not being a good enough father and husband. I slept around. I was mean to Zach when I should've been there for him. And . . . some other things."

There's this huge emptiness in me and I want to fill it. Those had been Tommy's words, and I repeat them now. "You were trying to fill your emptiness."

"Everyone deals with loss in their own way. You're going to make mistakes, just like I did. But eventually it will get better. Whatever you do wrong along the way, you have to go back and make amends. Or you'll never be able to live with yourself."

"Is that what you did? Made amends?"

He nods. "I'm still making them. Once you've hurt people, it's hard to fully gain their trust again. But closure's necessary for peace."

I don't know how to make amends. All I know how to do is

right the wrongs and trust in some cosmic way that my actions will negate my questionable ways.

Do I want to hurt the people I care most about? No, but I think it's inevitable. In the meantime I'll do everything I can to protect my family from the secrets, because any single one of them would crush those I love.

Closure for peace. My gut latches on to that statement. It makes logical sense. I thought I had closure when I purged myself of my mom's things. But now there's Marji.

She's a link I need to sever.

Chapter Twenty-Three

I ASK FOR SATURDAY OFF WORK AND HEAD straight to Richmond. I have no intentions of doing anything to Marji. Not today at least. But I do want to see her and where she lives. I want answers.

I keep an eye on my rearview on and off the whole way and am confident j_d_l is not trailing me. Traffic is hit or miss, and my GPS brings me to Marji's townhome some two hours later.

I park in the visitor section and sit for a bit just staring at her unit number. What exactly am I going to say to her? *I found a box of pictures. I saw you in the kill room. How many were you there for? Did you make me hurt that cat, or did I willingly do it?*

So many questions float in and out of my brain that I wish I had a pad and pen to write them all down.

Someone pulls into the spot beside me, and I blink out of my thoughts. I have no clue if she's home, but I get out of my Jeep and stand for a few more seconds as I continue staring up at her door.

I inhale a few nerve-fortifying breaths, and when I feel ready, I cross the parking lot and walk up her short driveway. Her garage door has a bank of windows, and I peek inside to see if a car is home.

A dark blue BMW stares back at me.

Son of a bitch. *She's* the one who has been following me? She's j_d_l? *She's* my copycat? That makes no sense at all.

I charge straight up her front stairs and ring the doorbell. A couple of seconds pass, and with each one my heart rate spikes.

Click. The dead bolt flips.

The door swings open, and my gut clenches at the sight of her. Immediately I'm filled with hate. Yes, it's the same woman as in the pictures, just older now. If she's my copycat, the cops are way off on the profile.

She gives me a long study before her lips curve up into a smile. "Lane."

Hearing the casual way she speaks my name unnerves me. "Marji."

She smiles even bigger. "I was wondering if you'd ever find out about me."

"You sent me a card. Obviously, I would."

She steps back and lets me in her house. "I'm sure you have a lot of questions. I know I do."

She leads me down a long hallway and into the kitchen. It occurs to me I should be scared, but I'm not. The hate is driving me. And the curiosity.

I sit down at the kitchen table, and while she pours me a cup of coffee, I notice her knife rack. She catches the glance and her lips twitch in amusement.

She hands me the coffee and takes a seat herself.

"Why have you been following me?" I launch right in.

She shrugs. "I've been following you all for quite a while now. Couple of months or so."

My jaw tightens.

"Daisy looks just like your mother." She takes in my angry expression and holds her hands up. "Don't worry. I'm not going to hurt anybody. I'm just curious."

"Well, stop it," I hiss. "Just stop it."

Marji nods. "Okay."

A few tense seconds go by, and I don't take my furious gaze off her. I want her to know I'm pissed. I also want her to know I *will* protect my family.

"I found a box of pictures and some letters," I tell her.

Marji brightens. "The letters?" She laughs. "Your mom and I got a kick out of being old-school pen pals." She laughs again. "Did you bring them with you?"

I'm repulsed. "No, I burned them."

She sighs, obviously upset over this statement.

"How did you know my parents?" I ask.

"Lane, I'm family. Your mom and I are *sisters*. I'm older by a year."

Sisters . . .

It takes me a second to wrap my brain around that.

How is it possible there is so much about my mother that I didn't know? How did I not know she had a sister? I don't get it. I just don't get it. *Hide in plain sight.* That's what Dr. Issa had said. It's exactly what my mother did. It's exactly what I'm doing.

Marji takes the cream and stirs it into her coffee. "I actually dated your father for a while. I introduced him to your mom."

My lip curls. If circumstances had been different Marji could've been my mother.

"Your mom and I used to talk all the time. I even babysat you on occasion, and then after she got married to Victor, I kept up with you through her. I have every one of your school pictures but this year, of course. Maybe you can send me one?"

She's got to be kidding.

She taps her spoon and sets it aside.

"Did you have any interaction with Daisy?" I ask.

Marji smiles again. I hate her smile. "Yes. It was all very sweet."

I don't believe her. "Did you think me and you skinning a cat was *sweet*, too?"

She chuckles and says, "Oh, Lane," and takes a sip of her coffee.

I want to grab her cup and smash it into her face.

"How did your mom really die?" she asks.

I choose to answer that question with one of my own. "How many of the killings were you there for?"

"About half of them."

"Did you participate or did you just watch?"

Her eyes brighten. "Oh, I definitely participated. I was even there for that one you witnessed too." She gets this faraway look on her face like she's remembering, and that look, almost one of fondness, sickens me. "Who knew all those animals we tortured when we were kids would transform into the greatness your mom became."

I stand up. I've heard enough. "You make me sick. What do you think this is? A friendly visit?" If only she knew what I'm capable of doing to her.

Marji reaches out and tenderly takes my hand. "Your mom was so quick to embrace things when we were kids. Just like you did."

I yank my hand from her creepy grasp. "I am *nothing* like my mother."

"Oh, but you really are."

I get right in her face. "You're part of this. You helped make me into who I am. *I hate you.*"

"I don't care who you are. I fully accept you." Marji closes the one-inch gap between us, and she kisses me on the cheek.

I rear back and punch her in the face.

My cell rings and it startles me. I don't know why, but I pull it out of my pocket and look. It's Dr. Issa. "What?" I snap into the phone.

"I heard you took the day off. Are you okay?"

"No."

He doesn't immediately respond, then, "Where are you?"

I look straight across the kitchen at Marji, my *aunt*, as she stares right back at me, smiling again.

Ugh.

"I'm fine." I click my phone off. "Are you JDL?"

She blinks. "I don't know what you're talking about."

"Of course you don't." I shove my phone in my pocket and walk straight past her out the front door. She's either lying or there are two people following me.

"See ya later," she yells after me, and I ignore her and whatever game she thinks she's playing.

As I peel out of her parking lot, I glance up to see her waving from her doorway.

I'm coming back for you, bitch.

Chapter Twenty-Four

I DRIVE LIKE A DEMON ON FIRE BACK UP I-95. I don't care if I get stopped. Bring it on. I weave in and out of traffic, get honked at, floor the gas, and push my Jeep to ninety. If I could, I'd drive off the end of the earth right now.

Mom and Marji are sisters. Deranged sisters. Victor has to know. Why wouldn't he have told me I have an aunt? Mom and Marji. Me and Daisy. Sisters.

Hell no, Daisy and I are nothing like them.

Marji said they stayed in contact. Did they meet in secret to what, talk about old times? Teach me to be like them? Teach Daisy?

Oh God.

I don't get it. None of this makes sense.

Why—why—*WHY* lead this life with kids and Victor? Was it some master plan—all for a cover so she could live this other crazy existence?

Did Mom intend for me to find those pictures? She intended for me to be the next Decapitator, this I know. But what were her intentions with Daisy? What, she had two daughters and thought, *Let me see which one is the darkest*?

So if she and Marji had been hurting animals and doing their evil stuff way before they met my real dad, then she'd been planning on this for years. Her first kill hadn't been a crime of passion, like she claimed. Who's to say my preschool teacher was her first kill? She and Marji could've very well butchered a person before that. She and Marji could've practiced on several people for all I know.

Panic ricochets through me as I grip my steering wheel and do something I never do. I scream.

A semi driver blares his horn. I yank my Jeep right in front of him and slam on my brakes. He slams on his and skids, and I gun my engine to take the Falls Church exit. Horns echo after me, and I clench my teeth in need. If I could kill someone right now, I would.

I totally get why Tommy comes out here on his bike and drives the way he does. It's reckless and stupid. I'm fully aware of this. But it's an out for the anger scorching my insides.

I can't go home. I need something . . . *now*.

I drive the back roads to—I'm not sure where. Find myself in Seven Corners, then in the parking lot of an apartment complex I know of but have never actually been to.

I climb from my Jeep, slam my door, and take the outside steps two at a time. I find the apartment I'm looking for and bang on the door.

It swings open and I don't wait for a welcome; I just charge right on in.

"Lane, what are you doing here?" Dr. Issa cautiously asks. "How did you know where I live?"

"Zach told me." I turn on him. "Who *am I*?"

"What's wrong? What happened?"

"I just found out . . ."

He waits.

My mind reels with the enormity of it all, and I want to tell him. I *need* to tell him. "I just found out my mom has a sister and was hiding *a lot* of secrets from me."

Dr. Issa doesn't even blink. "What secrets?"

I stare into his dark eyes, sink into them, really. What am I doing? I have to get in control. I can't tell him who I am. Who my mom was. Marji. My real dad. The pictures. What am I doing? I grab my head. I have to stop thinking. I have to focus.

I close my eyes. *Aarrgghh . . .*

"Lane?"

My eyes snap open, and whatever he sees in them makes him step back.

"You need to leav—"

I launch myself at him, cover his mouth with my own, press my body to his. Somewhere in the far depths of my brain I'm aware he's resisting, but I don't stop.

He turns and pushes me against the wall, and everywhere in my brain it now registers he's no longer resisting.

I wrap my legs around him and he grinds against me. I dig my fingers into his hair and he rips my coat open. I shove him back onto the couch, straddle him, and ride his erection right into climax. I cry out. Then he does. And we both fall limply against each other.

I swallow, my eyes closed, every cell in my body vibrating in numb pulses.

I don't know how much time passes, but I finally open my eyes to see him gently pushing me off him.

He scrubs his hands down his face. "I can't believe that just happened."

I slowly, *carefully*, get to my feet. I tune in to myself and realize my brain is completely, blessedly, empty. "I needed that."

He looks up at me from the couch. "That can't happen again."

"I know." He's twenty-five. I'm seventeen. I know.

Dr. Issa glances at the open door. And sighs. "God, I didn't realize that was open."

I look down at my clothes, only now realizing that other than my jacket neither one of us unbuttoned, unzipped, un-nothinged. Both of our jeans are fully intact.

"I'm going to go." I don't wait for a response and instead walk right out the open door, down to my Jeep, and climb back inside.

My phone rings. Zach. Talk about a shitty coincidence. "Hey."

"I wasn't sure you'd answer."

I put my key in and crank my engine.

"What are you doing?" he asks.

Humping your brother. "On my way home. Did you need something?"

Zach doesn't respond. So much time goes by that I check my phone, see we're still connected, and prompt, "Zach?"

He sighs. "No, I guess not. Sorry. Bye."

He clicks off and I consider calling back but dial Dr. Issa instead. He doesn't pick up, which doesn't surprise me. It rolls to voice mail and I simply say, "Zach just called me. He doesn't sound good. Check on him."

I drive straight home, and despite the call from Zach, my brain still stays pleasantly empty. No spinning thoughts. No urges to curb. It seems orgasms from the Issa brothers might be the key to maintaining my sanity.

This thought has me smiling to myself as I walk the side-walk to our front door.

"Hey."

I glance up to see Tommy sitting on his motorcycle. I immediately think of that kiss on my cheek. His whiskers. And get turned on imagining what would've happened if I'd visited him instead of Dr. Issa.

He studies me for a second. "I've never seen you smile before."

"Nor I you."

Tommy nods at that. "Point taken."

"How did you know where I live?"

"Went to Patch and Paw and asked. They told me."

"They're not to supposed to tell you that information."

Tommy shrugs. "I know. I was surprised. Anyway, I wanted to apologize."

"For?"

"Last time. I feel like I might have accused you or blamed you or something."

"You didn't. We're good."

He glances at my front door, and I get the distinct impression he didn't come to apologize. "I get it," I decide to tell him. "The crazy driving. I did it today. It makes sense now."

"No it doesn't. It's stupid."

"True. It is. But I get it." I'm fully aware I don't have to tell him this, but something inside me says he needs to hear it.

"Thanks."

Our front door opens and Gramps steps out. He looks down the steps at us. First me, then Tommy. "Dinner's on. Who's your friend?"

My gramps really does annoy me. "Tommy. He's in my grief group."

This seems to appease him. "Five minutes."

I want to tell him to get started without me, but I know this'll press my luck. "Okay."

Gramps closes the door, and a VW Bug pulls up. It double parks and Catalina steps out. Marji, Dr. Issa, Zach, Tommy, and now Catalina all in one day. Suddenly my blessedly calm brain isn't so tranquil.

She waves—"Lane"—then glances at Tommy. "Hey. What are *you* doing here?"

I look between them. "You two know each other?"

He doesn't answer and instead cranks his engine and drives off.

O-kay. That was rude.

Catalina steps onto the sidewalk. "Yeah, we know each other. He used to be a pretty active member on the Masked Savior site."

Isn't this interesting? "He's not on anymore?"

She shakes her head. "Not for a while now."

Huh. Tommy used to be a member of "my" site. Why would he have stopped posting?

"But anyway, I was driving past your neighborhood and thought I'd stop in and tell you something."

I raise my brows, waiting.

"I heard my dad talking on the phone. Someone's come forward claiming the Masked Savior abducted him, but he escaped, *and* he saw who the Savior really is."

Chapter Twenty-Five

"WHICH ONE?" I ASK. "THE REAL OR THE copycat?"

She scrunches her nose up. "I don't know. But—"

Gramps comes back out the door. "Dinner," he annoyingly reminds me.

I fight the urge to roll my eyes.

"Listen, I'll call you later," Catalina promises.

Reluctantly I go inside and sit through dinner, but all I can think about is what Catalina said. Someone's come forward and can identify the Masked Savior. Or rather my copycat. Because *I* certainly didn't abduct anybody.

By eleven p.m. she still irritatingly has not called, and I'm not about to dial her. That would come across as too needy.

I get my laptop instead and do a general search on *Masked Savior* and come up with a zillion links for people who want to hire me.

Bizarre.

I lie awake most of the night going through the time line. Who I used to be, where I started, what I came from, where I am now. I cycle through this over and over and decide, at this point, I just need to know who this person is who claims he escaped and can identify "me." He's the only viable link to my copycat.

My natural inclination is to text Reggie, as Catalina has proven to be unreliable, but of course I don't.

The entire next day goes by, and I finally hear from Catalina via text right before dinner. GUY THAT CAME FWD IS MICHAEL MASON. DON'T KNOW WHO HE IDENTIFIED AS SAVIOR.

Michael Mason? Doesn't sound familiar. THANKS. I text her back, and immediately plug his name into a search engine. Ex-military, been in jail a couple of times for petty theft, but nothing huge. He was questioned and released and doesn't appear to be a hardened criminal.

Definitely not my type.

I copy his address down anyway and make a plan for a visit. I'm going to see what he does and doesn't know.

Our doorbell rings and Daisy runs to get it. "Hammond!" She pulls him inside. "We're just sitting down to dinner." She glances over her shoulder. "Dad, can Hammond stay?"

"Sure," he agrees. "It's just spaghetti, but there's plenty."

We all sit down, the perfect family we are, and I can't help but get a little soft at Daisy and Hammond. They really are sweet.

"So"—Gramps gazes right at me—"where were you yesterday? You didn't go to your Patch and Paw shift."

My entire family glances up. I've never missed a shift.

"You're right. I took the day off. I wanted to be by myself." I look my grandfather dead in the eyes. "How is it, exactly, that you know I didn't do my shift?"

"I just happened to be driving by and stopped in to say hi."

Yeah, right.

Gramps narrows his eyes, ever so slightly. "So where were you?"

I turn from him to Victor, because, well, I answer to him, not my grandfather. "I drove around, Dad. Got a little lost. Took some time to think. Saw a friend. That's it."

Victor's expression softens. "That's okay. Better now?"

"Yes." I want to look back at my grandfather but don't. He *won't* come between me and my family.

A few quiet seconds tick by, then Daisy whispers something to Hammond, he laughs, and things seem back to normal. I still don't look at Gramps. But I *know* he's staring at me.

"I heard," Gramps starts in again, "that the FBI will take over this Masked Savior business if the local task force can't figure things out. Something about vigilante terrorism?"

Victor glances around the table, clearly uncomfortable talking business in front of us kids. "At this point there're way too many things up in the air. So, Justin . . ." And with that Victor expertly diverts the conversation.

Vigilante terrorism. FBI stepping in. Yes, I need to get this figured out. Because the last thing I need is the FBI on my ass. This local task force is pain enough.

As I'm doing dishes, I get a call from Zach. "Hey," I answer.

"Hey, you."

I smile.

"Sorry about the call. Everything's okay, in case you were worried or something."

"I was," I say, realizing I honestly am and wishing I would've thought to check in with him before now.

"My brother called me and, well, all is fine."

So Dr. Issa got my message. Good.

"Anyway, that's all."

I want to keep him on the phone but really don't know what to say, so I decide on "Bye, Zach," and truly hope he's okay.

Chapter Twenty-Six

THE NEXT NIGHT GRAMPS IS OUT WITH SOME friend, so it's easy for me to say to Victor, "Off to the coffee shop to study."

"Be back by midnight." He gives his obligatory comment, to which I nod.

I keep a careful eye on my rearview and am certain I'm not being trailed. By seven thirty I'm sitting outside Michael Mason's apartment complex several blocks from the Reston Town Center.

People come and go, and no one notices me in the packed parking lot. Just the way I like it. Michael lives on the first floor, and a little before nine his front door opens and he steps out dressed in all black. I know from what I looked up that he's thirty-one, divorced, and has no children. I give him a good, long study, and, no, I definitely don't know this guy.

He zips up his dark jacket, climbs onto a bicycle, and pedals out of the complex.

I follow.

He goes down the road about a mile and pulls into a nearby park. I give my surroundings another long look, still certain no one is trailing me, and park my Jeep near a few other cars. Michael doesn't even glance up as he locks his bike to a rack and enters a trail.

It's near black out, and I give myself a second to take in the area. Over in the far field there's a group of guys playing moon-light football. Maybe Michael is here for the game.

I climb from my Jeep, and as I enter the path Michael took, I pull my ski mask down.

He strolls along, oblivious, and I come right up on him.

He turns at the exact same second, clearly sensing me, and then fully faces me.

I pause. *O-kay.* Not expecting that.

His eyes go wide. "It's you!"

I don't respond.

"You're the *real* Masked Savior, aren't you?"

I concentrate on keeping my voice low and manly. "You claim to have been held and released by the Masked Savior. Claim to have seen him. Describe him." Describe my copycat.

He studies me for a second. "Are you here to thank me?"

What? Thank him. Thank him for what? "Describe him," I repeat instead, puzzling at why he doesn't seemed scared of me.

"I believe in you. I *am* you. Everything I've done, it's for the mission."

The mission?

"Don't worry. I gave the police the description I was told."

Told?

"Average height, average weight, dark hair, dark eyes."

That goes against every other Savior description. Why would he have been told to do that? And by whom?

He chuckles. "We really threw the task force off with that one."

"Who is 'we'?" I ask.

"That whore," he continues, not answering my question. "I gladly did what I had to."

What is he talking about? What whore? The teenage prostitute?

"She deserved to die."

Die? Wait a minute. People have been beaten to near death, but no one has actually died.

"Were you sent to thank me?" He repeats his prior question.

I don't respond.

His face brightens. "You were, weren't you?"

Realization gradually settles in. This guy doesn't know anything. Whatever "whore" he's talking about is someone other than the teen prostitute. No wonder this guy was questioned and released by the cops. "You didn't really see the Masked Savior did you?" He didn't really see my copycat.

This man, Michael Mason, is a fraud. He wasn't captured and able to identify anybody. He's just some twisted fan of the Masked Savior.

He snorts. "No, I didn't really see the Masked Savior." Then he grins. "But I do now. You're right here!"

This guy's got nothing I need. He's meant to throw not only the task force off, but probably me, too.

Except he's actually murdered someone in my name. Why don't I know about this woman he killed? Did it not make the news? Though I doubt he had anything to do with the teen prostitute, the homeless boy, and Jacks, I still ask him about them.

"What? No," he answers. "I'm a stabber. I'm not a beater. I stabbed that whore. I dumped her body right in these woods. They haven't even found her yet." Michael laughs like that's the funniest thing ever.

This man is insane.

"I'm still waiting for my thank-you," he says.

"You were told to pretend you were taken by the Masked Savior?"

He nods.

"Who told you?"

"I can't tell you that."

I take a patient breath. "Does JDL mean anything to you?"

He scrunches his face up and thinks. "Who's that?"

All I want to do is beat information out of him, but I know he won't respond to that. "Did the same person who told you to pretend tell you to kill this 'whore'?"

He giggles. "No, that was all me. I'll take you to the body. Do you want to see?"

"Yes." *Then I'll taser and zip-tie you and turn your sick ass in.*

Michael turns and strolls off. "Okay, follow me."

I stay a careful distance behind, my senses on full alert. He starts talking, but it's not to me. He's carrying on a conversation with his own self.

This man is unbalanced. For sure. Mentally, something is off. He will definitely pay for what he's done to this woman. Either in prison or a mental institution.

He leaves the trail. "It's just over here."

I watch as he makes his way through the dark woods, and I get my Taser out and ready. In the moonlight I still see him and I take another second to stop, survey the area, and tune in to my senses. Myself.

Everything in me tells me this guy is really leading me to a body. This isn't some sort of trap.

He stops at a huge mound of dirty snow that looks recently piled. He doesn't point, just looks.

I look too and don't see anything.

Michael leans down, grabs something, and tugs, and out from beneath the pile a dirty and bloody woman's body emerges.

Without a hesitant second I lift my Taser and shoot. He drops to the ground with a high-pitched scream that sends a tiny bit of blood surging in my veins.

While he spasms into a twitchy mess, I wrangle his wrists together and zip-tie them. Then I do his thighs and ankles.

His twitching becomes more violent, spit foams in the corners of his mouth, and I realize something's not right. He's having a seizure.

I take a step back as his body lashes to the right and back to the left, and then his eyes snap open to stare up at the dark sky. He lets out a long, throaty moan before going completely still.

I suck in a sharp breath. What the hell. . . . He's not dead, is he? I study his open eyes, his neck where there *isn't* a pulse, and his chest that is *not* rising with breath.

Oh. My. God.

I stand in disbelief staring down at his body, and then I quickly move, kneeling to get a closer look.

There. It's faint, but it's there. A raspy breath. I press my fingers to his neck, not expecting to feel a pulse through my gloves, but trying anyway.

There. Another raspy breath. He's alive!

I blow out a relieved breath and stare at his chest, watching as he inhales another hesitant breath. Why? Why do I care if this deranged man is alive?

Because he killed someone for me. The Masked Savior. Or for his twisted view of the Savior. Obviously, he's mentally unbalanced, but he killed an innocent person in my name.

I'm disgusted. And angry. How did this all get so out of control? How did my own dark urges spiral into this bizarre fan club?

This all started with me. This is my fault. It has to end.

He said someone told him. Who—my copycat? j_d_l? Because what if they aren't the same? What if j_d_l and my copycat are actually two different people? Either way, I have to stop this. This right here proves it is much bigger than I realized.

I dig his cell from his front pocket and dial 911. The stabbed woman moans and I jump back. She's alive too? Holy shit!

"What is your emergency?" I hear over the cell.

My pulse kicks in as I drop the phone and sprint back through the frozen woods. I dive into my Jeep and get the hell out of the park.

A mile down the road I hear sirens and exhale a long breath.

She's alive. Thank God, she's alive, and so is Michael Mason.

Then how come neither thought alleviates my guilt?

Chapter Twenty-Seven

THE NEXT DAY I GOOGLE MICHAEL MASON and the unidentified woman. She's currently in a hospital, and he's in a psych ward. She was able to describe the horror of her ordeal, but she did not see who tasered and zip-tied Mason.

I cruise my news feeds next, and the whole event, of course, is being connected to the Masked Savior. Because of the tasering and zip ties.

So much for laying low. The night did not go as I expected. But what was I supposed to do? Let the woman die in the woods and Michael go free? Absolutely not.

It's all I can think about as I drive to my grief group meeting. When I arrive, my phone rings. It's Catalina. "Yeah?" I answer.

"Michael Mason's in a psych ward," she whispers.

Michael Mason is exactly where he belongs. He's going to get some much-needed help. I don't say this though and instead respond, "Why are you whispering?"

"I don't want my dad to hear. Did you tell anyone about Michael being the only eyewitness to the Masked Savior?"

"No, you?"

She pauses. "Just Kyle. Everyone on the task force obviously knows. Dad says there're always leaks. It's almost impossible to contain information. He was so pissed when Michael Mason popped up zip-tied. But he's also pissed Mason's description doesn't fit their already compiled profile of the Savior."

Good. That's good. Keep the local task force guessing. I wait for Catalina to bring up the stabbed woman, but she doesn't.

"Catalina, I wanted to run a thought by you."

"Okay, shoot."

"You and I both think there's a real Masked Savior and a copycat. Do you think the copycat is acting on his or her own, or do you think there's another person involved?" *Like j_d_l.*

"Um . . . nah. I think the copycat is acting on his own."

"Do you think the copycat is a member of the Masked Savior site?"

"Totally," she immediately answers. "I cruise the posts all the time trying to figure out which one it is."

Which validates my previous thought that j_d_l and the copycat *are* one and the same. "Any ideas?" *Please say j_d_l.*

"There're a lot of weirdos on the site. Honestly, could be any of them."

"You're the site administrator. Do you ever look at the records and see who is who?" I hold my breath and hope she says yes so I can probe her more about j_d_l.

"M's the only one with access to everything—you know, IPs and all. Plus I'm sure a lot of people give fake registrations like you did."

"M?"

"The creator of the site."

"Huh." I guess I thought since Catalina was the administrator, she was also the creator. "How did you end up the administrator?"

She laughs. "I filled out an application. M picked me."

"You ever met this M?"

"No. To my knowledge Tommy's the only one who has. He's the only one who knows M's true identity."

Tommy . . . of course.

I hang up with her and head inside. I sit through grief group, but I don't hear a word. I'm too focused on Tommy and how I'm going to broach the subject.

When group is over, I head straight toward him. "Can we talk?"

"Okay."

I follow him outside. Some of the other group members wave good-bye, and as soon as we're alone, I turn to him. "You used to be an active member of the Masked Savior site."

His expression doesn't change. "Catalina told you that?"

"Yes."

"Are *you* on it?" he counters.

"Sort of. I registered and then took it down. I still look at it every so often though. Catalina said you took your registration down too?"

"That's correct."

I wait for him to elaborate, but of course he doesn't. "Will you tell me why?"

Tommy's blue eyes bore deeply into mine. "Yes. I'll answer whatever other questions you have too. But first, I want you to share something with me that I don't know."

I don't like this. "Like what?"

"You decide. Make it good."

If I "make it good," he'll tell me what I'm fishing to know. I get it. The obvious things pop into my mind: My mom was the Decapitator; I'm the Masked Savior. But I choose instead: "I recently found out my mom has a sister I never knew about." Good, but not too gritty. It's the same thing I told Dr. Issa.

Tommy slips his keys from his jacket pocket, walks over, and climbs on his bike, making it obvious that wasn't good enough.

I take a step toward him, my heart suddenly pounding, knowing exactly what I'm about to say. "I was there fourteen years ago when my uncle killed his first victim. I saw the whole thing."

Tommy doesn't climb off his bike. He stays straddling it, staring at me.

I hold his stare, unexpectedly feeling lighter, *freer*, for sharing more truth with him than I have ever with anyone else. Even if it is a truth hidden in lies.

"I knew you were hiding something. I could tell."

I don't like that at all. The very last thing I need is someone to be able to read me and the things I'm hiding. "Why aren't you on the Masked Savior site anymore?"

"Because the creator of the site contacted me personally and wanted me to do things I wasn't comfortable doing."

My pulse thumps. "Like what?"

"Things."

I try not to get frustrated. "Why did you join?"

"I was looking for . . . something."

An out, I'm sure, to his grief. "You didn't find it?"

"No."

"I know the creator of the site," I lie, hoping to move this conversation in the direction I need it to go. "M."

He doesn't seem surprised at all. "Do you now?"

I don't respond, and I get the distinct impression he knows I'm lying. Now I regret I did.

Tommy cranks his engine. "That lie just cost you this conversation. See you later." With that he rides off, and I turn and kick the lamppost. *Shit!*

He was going to tell me something. He *was*. And I ruined it. I ruined it!

Chapter Twenty-Eight

WHEN I GET HOME, I PULL UP "MY" SITE AND start scrolling. It's buzzing about Michael Mason's encounter with the Masked Savior.

[VodkaRocks] *There's the Savior we love!*

[j_d_l] *Welcome back. So much for laying low.*

I narrow my eyes. There you are, j_d_l. You've been laying low as well. I hover my mouse over his avatar, and he immediately begins typing again.

[j_d_l] *What are your darkest desires?*

Right now? To meet this M person and to also figure out who you are. But my darkest desire? To kill Marji.

Wait a minute . . . M. *Marji*. Hell freaking A. There's no way they could be one and the same. My mom knew I was the

Masked Savior, and she probably told Marji. Marji's a psycho, but she wouldn't lower herself to something like developing a fan site. Would she?

[KyleScienceGuy] My darkest desire is to see Junior's legs broken.

It's the first response that pops up to j_d_l's question, and I sit back in my chair. *Whoa.* O-kay. Not what I expected to read from Kyle, Science Club President. By Junior, I assume he means our homecoming king. Sure, Junior's a dick, and I've seen him push Kyle around a time or two, but broken legs? That's a bit much.

I read a few more responses to the darkest desire question. The majority of them want to get back at someone for something. Not good.

Here's the thing: I know this is a fan site, but Catalina's right. There are a lot of weirdos registered. People like Michael Mason, who would branch out and do things to others. The people on this site don't just talk about the Masked Savior, they fantasize about hurting others. The task force is supposedly monitoring the site, they're reading this stuff. They're tracking it.

I want to log on and IM j_d_l again, but I'm just not confident I can do it without being traced. I hover my mouse over j_d_l's avatar once more, and a few seconds later he logs off.

My phone rings. Catalina. "Hey."

"You're not going to believe this," she excitedly whispers. "M contacted me."

My blood twitches. "For?"

"Not sure. I'll find out soon. God, this is so exciting. The Masked Savior has inspired *so* many of us. We're all becoming friends."

I immediately think of what Tommy said. "Are you meeting in person?"

"No, we're having a phone conversation." She lowers her voice even more. "If I can arrange it, would you like to virtually meet M too?"

Inside I smirk. "Yes. Definitely."

She laughs. "Ha! I adore you. You've got a little dark side too." She has no idea.

"Okay, that's it. Gotta go. Bye."

"Bye." I hang up and just sit for a bit, going through everything. The Weasel—the rapist. Marco—the animal abuser. Heather—the drunk driver. All things I did before Mom.

The shaved cheerleader. Aisha—the druggie. Michael—the deranged stabber. All things I did after Mom.

Then I cycle through all the ones I didn't actually do: the teen prostitute; the homeless boy; Jacks, who I wanted to do but didn't.

The cops have a profile. Michael Mason gave them a different one. I think it's time I confused them a little more.

I've been on the defense, like my aikido training has taught me. What if I were to go on the offense? Compose a statement to the local task force, detailing everything I know, not using names, but all the inside information. That, coupled with a false profile, might just be the key to leading the task force in a different direction and buying me more time to figure all this out.

I know exactly who I'm going to point them to.

Chapter Twenty-Nine

THE NEXT AFTERNOON I WALK INTO THE bathroom I share with my brother and sister and grab my toothbrush. Daisy is standing at the other sink, putting on mascara and slowly swaying to whatever's playing in her ears.

I brush my teeth as I watch her. . . . Normally, she's rocking out to indie punk.

She catches me looking and smiles, then plucks one bud from her ear and slips it into mine. It's acoustical guitar. Huh.

"Hammond introduced me to it. Nice, isn't it?"

I nod and continue brushing my teeth. Then I pile my curls into a ponytail, all the while listening with her. She's right. Nice. Peaceful.

The song ends and she slips the bud from my ear. "What happened to you and Zach?"

Wasn't expecting that question. "There really wasn't ever a 'me and Zach.'"

She gives me a soft smile that is nothing like the sister I used to know. "Yes there was. Whether you want to admit it or not. He's good for you." Playfully she punches my arm. "And you were good for him, too."

No, I wasn't. I'm not good for anybody. "Heading to Patch and Paw. See you later."

She gives me a wave. "Yep, later."

As I walk out our front door, I see Tommy propped on his bike. The last thing he called me was a liar. He's not exactly the person I want to see right now.

"I have been researching the Decapitator nonstop since I found out you were his niece," he begins, with no niceties at all. "Nowhere in that research did I find any mention of you witnessing the first killing."

I don't respond. I don't know what he expects me to say. Everything surrounding the Decapitator is hidden deep. Very few people know, in an official capacity, that I was found at three years old in the same room where my preschool teacher had been violently murdered.

"I suppose it has everything to do with your parents working for the FBI."

He supposes right.

"What I want to know is, how disturbed did it make you?"

My heart pauses midbeat at his question, but I don't answer.

"My guess is it made you question your whole existence."

I don't like how close he's getting. He's reading me a little too well. "You don't know what you're talking about." Even I can hear the defensiveness in my tone.

"Oh, I think I do."

I swallow, and he follows the nervous movement with his eyes. It pisses me off.

"I said before, I think you're hiding something." He cranks his engine. "I still do." With that he pulls off.

What the hell was that, and how exactly does he expect me to respond? He thinks he can come and go, be confrontational, be cryptic, and challenge me. How wrong he is. Tommy needs to take a step back out of my business.

That night I get home from my Patch and Paw shift to find Gramps and Justin working on a model.

"Justin, you're not doing it right. Are you not listening to me?" Gramps demands.

"I'm sorry," my brother mumbles. "I'm trying."

Gramps sighs. "I don't know why you asked me to help if you planned on doing it your own way."

Justin ducks his head and sniffs and I lose it. "Leave him alone."

Gramps swerves his head toward me. "Young lady, you do *not* talk to me that way."

"And you don't talk to my brother that way."

"Your *half* brother."

I take a step toward him and Gramps stands up.

"It's okay," Justin intercedes.

The old man and I stare each other down for a few long seconds, and he turns away first. I grab my stuff and charge upstairs.

"Hey," Victor greets me from his room. "Time to talk?"

"Sure."

"Let's go for a walk."

Oh . . . strange. Why would Victor want to go for a walk? This isn't like him. At all. It kind of freaks me out.

We pass Gramps on the way back out, and I don't even glance in his direction.

Outside and down the dark sidewalk, Victor speaks. "I feel like we never get any time together. How are you doing?"

I give my standard response. "Fine."

Victor wraps his arm around me, and the warmth feels so good in the cold night. "Lane, you can talk to me."

He needs something, I realize this, and so I conjure up enough truth for meaning. "I . . . feel like my life is a lie. That our family is the only thing keeping me sane." I pause a second to formulate what I want to say next. "I don't know what I would do if it went away. Some days I seem like myself, and others I don't recognize me."

He smiles gently. "I feel the same way," he quietly admits. "Some days I walk around in a daze wondering where things go from here. I really miss your mom."

I want so badly to tell him Mom wasn't the woman he loved, but that's a burden only I'll carry. Justin, Daisy, and Victor will remember the fictitious version of her.

We round the block and continue in silence. Then Victor goes on, "I know you need an 'out' for your anger, your confusion, your questions. . . ."

I stop walking and turn to him. "What are you talking about?"

"I know you've been on that Masked Savior website."

What? How does he know that?

"I'm asking you, no, *telling* you, to stay off of it. This vigilante thing has gotten out of hand. The task force is on that site, routinely cruising the feeds, keeping records on everything. Just stay off of it, okay?"

Has Catalina's father had this same talk with her?

"Dad, how do you know I've been on the site?"

"Quite by accident, I assure you. Your brother was using my laptop, so I grabbed yours and stumbled across it."

I believe him. He's always respected my privacy. He's never been the type to snoop. Now if it were Gramps . . .

"Thank you," I honestly tell him. "And I will. No more website. I promise."

Victor hugs me. "Exactly what I wanted to hear. Also"—he starts walking me back to our house—"how well have you gotten to know Catalina?"

"A little well. Why?"

Victor takes a deep breath, like he's trying to figure out how to say what he wants to say. "Catalina's father shared something with me that I think you need to know."

This doesn't sound good. "When Catalina was a little girl, she fell down their stairs and was in a coma for a while. She sustained frontal-lobe damage from that fall."

I stop walking. "What are you trying to tell me?"

"According to her father, it affected her processing, her moods, impulsivity, and her behaviors. She does things and doesn't think they're wrong. That's why she's been home-schooled. She used to have a lot of problems with other kids. You've heard the term 'doesn't play well with others.' Well, that's how he described Catalina."

Interesting.

"I'm telling you because I want you to be careful with her. She's intelligent, astute, and, as I just mentioned, struggles with processing and impulsivity issues. Her dad says she's really developed over the years, made progress with her doctors, but still, be alert. Okay?"

"Okay."

We walk back to our house, and all I can puzzle about is Catalina. Processing. Impulsivity. Moody. Save for the intelligence, I haven't seen any of those other things in her. I know I've been a little off, but not so much that I would've misread her, right?

Chapter Thirty

THAT NIGHT AS I GO TO SLEEP, MY MIND
shifts to Tommy. What does he know about this leader, M, and
what has he discovered in his research of the Decapitator?
Honestly, if Reggie really put her mind to it, she could likely dig
up things I never want dug up again. If *I* had Reggie's skills, I
would find everything I could and permanently delete it.

What I can try to do is figure out Tommy's level of exper-
tise. . . .

In the morning I head downstairs and hear Victor and Gramps
already up and in the kitchen.

"She was disrespectful to me," Gramps harshly whispers.

I pause to listen.

Victor sighs. "You have *always* ridden Lane harder than the other two. Ease up on my daughter."

"She's not your daughter," Gramps snaps.

That comment pierces straight through me like a hot, sad knife.

"Yes. She. Is," Victor defends me.

"I've noticed Justin is starting to get out of hand. You've lost control of your kids."

I hear Victor pace away, pause, then walk back. "We haven't been doing great, but we're doing okay. We're getting there as a family. The kids were obviously happy to see you, but it's come to enough. When you make my son cry, it's enough."

"Did Lane tell you that?" Gramps retorts.

"No, *Dad*, Daisy did. Listen, I appreciate you coming, but it's best if you go back home now."

Gramps doesn't immediately respond. "You mark my words, that *daughter* of yours . . . she's going to cause you nothing but trouble."

Even though I've heard him say this before, it still hurts.

"No, she's not. She's perfect in her own unique way. I want you gone by the end of the day."

As quietly as I can, I tiptoe back up the stairs to my room. I close my door, lie down on my bed, and think about my grandfather. Maybe he shares that inner sense that I do. He knows something's not right with me.

A note on my desk catches my attention. I glance over and see it's from Justin.

WILL you COME TO THE ART FAIR?
My MODEL WILL BE ON DISPLAY.
IT'S TODAY AFTER SCHOOL.
DAISY SAID SHE'D COME.

I smile and grab a pen. *YES!* I write back and go tape it on his door. Gramps is out of here. Victor loves me. Daisy really is a sister. And Justin wants me to come to his art fair.

My family. My sanity. As long as I have them, my world will be all right.

After school I look up Tommy and find his name connected to his sister, of course, the Decapitator's victim. I also find him buried in several links throughout middle and high school. I select a few of them. He went to Longfellow Middle and then on to Thomas Jefferson High. I click through more links to awards he received in . . . computer science.

Great.

I think you're hiding something.

Why would he say that to me? Just to taunt?

I sit for a second and consider what story I might be able to tell Reggie so she'll help me find out if Tommy knows more than I think he does. I come up with several and decide on none. I'm falling into old patterns, and this isn't how I want to become friends with Reggie again.

I'm just going to have to break into Tommy's apartment and do some digging.

"Ready?" Daisy asks.

I close down the library's computer and dig my Jeep keys out, and we head to Justin's art fair. This is something my mom would've gone to. It occurs to me—this is the first school thing Justin's done without her.

Daisy must think this too, because she hugs Justin and says, "Mom would be very proud."

I hug him too. "She would."

He grins. "Thanks."

That grin is all I need to promise myself I'll go to every one of his things after this.

While the judges walk around, I hang along the back wall and watch it all. To the left I spy Kyle near his sister's display, standing, glaring across the room. I follow that glare to see I-want-to-break-his-legs Junior.

Holy goddamn hell—he's on crutches with a cast covering his entire left leg.

I glance back to Kyle to see him staring right at me. His glare softens, like he's trying to hide it, and he turns to his sister.

What did he do to Junior?

I walk right toward Kyle and pull him aside. I don't bother telling him I saw his post on the site. I don't bother telling him the cops are monitoring said site. I merely say, "Tell me you're not responsible for that."

"I don't know what you're talking about." He feigns innocence. "I heard Junior fell down some stairs."

Yeah, right. I *know* this isn't my fight, and yes, Junior's a dick, but a broken leg? Jesus. "I trust Junior won't be falling down any more stairs?" I venture.

Kyle shrugs. "Depends on how clumsy he is."

Oh, no, this isn't going to work for me. But I started all this. I inadvertently gave a green light to my "fan club" to go out and wreak havoc. Now I have to clean up their mess, stop them, redirect them, something. . . .

Plus, I know that look in Kyle's eyes. Now that he's had a taste of violence, he's ready for a little more. I've created a monster of a problem.

This is why I value my solitude. Fan clubs, gangs, followings—it's too many people. Too much everything.

The thing is, I've spent my whole life the way I am. I'm used to it. It's me. It's my innate being. The rest of these fools are taking risks. They're careless, thoughtless, and lack direction, and *hopefully* will screw up and get caught.

Hopefully.

A honking horn has me glancing past Kyle, through the

bank of windows and out into the parking lot, where a dark blue BMW sits.

Marji smiles and waves, and I narrow my eyes. What is she doing?

"Who's that?" Daisy asks, and I spin to block her line of sight. I didn't realize she walked up.

"I don't know," I tell her. "Probably a parent, someone Mom knew."

I take Daisy's arm and steer her away. When we're back near Justin, I glance over my shoulder to see Marji gone.

Chapter Thirty-One

MARJI'S TAUNTING ME. I WILL DEAL WITH her. But first I want to see if Tommy knows more than I think he does about the Decapitator, and how, if at all, he is still connected to this M person.

Through my cyber digging I discover he lives alone in the basement apartment of someone's house. He attends afternoon classes and works at Whole Foods at night.

I drive by Whole Foods to make sure his bike is there and then head to his apartment.

I pull my mask down, slip my gloves on, and give the area one last look. All clear.

Victor taught me how to pick a lock. All for fun of course, but I use the skill to let myself into Tommy's place.

I have one hour until he gets home from work.

His stove light is on, and I stand in the doorway to orient myself. Clean. Smells like Clorox wipes. Sparsely decorated. Studio. One TV. One bed. An oversize chair. Small kitchen. A few other things here and there.

Exactly the type of place I can see myself in someday.

I spy his laptop on the bed, go straight to it, and take it. Beside his chair sits a backpack. I unzip, dig around, find a few thumb drives, and take those, too. Then I start at his closet and make my way through his entire apartment. I open boxes, go through drawers, riffle through files and papers. I find only one large envelope full of clippings about the Decapitator and take that as well.

I check my watch. Fifteen minutes.

I grab it all up, head out the door, walk down the block, climb in my Jeep, and am gone. He'll probably assume it's a robbery and call the cops. That's fine. I'll have his stuff dumped in no time.

I pull over in an empty parking lot and crank up his laptop. It's not password protected, and I go straight to Search and type in *DECAPITATOR*. About a zillion documents pop up. I'm no computer science expert, but I do know enough to understand that even if I wipe these, there are still ways to retrieve them. Plus, he's already read them all.

I also do a quick search of his files on Marji's full name and get nothing. I do the Masked Savior next and get nothing on that as well. If he's been lying and he is still connected to the group, he's wiped the files that link his participation.

I find everything I can regarding his university classwork and personal things like pictures, and I transfer it all to an empty flash drive of my own.

I drive straight to Patch and Paw, let myself in, go to the crematorium room, and burn it all: his laptop, the file, the drives, the Decapitator. . . . I know metal doesn't burn all the way down, but his stuff will be charred enough.

The room fills with the pungent scent of burning plastic, and I wrinkle my nose.

I'll use my savings to buy him a new laptop, and send it to him along with the personal stuff I transferred.

I empty the crematory, and as I head from Patch and Paw, my phone rings. I don't recognize the number. "Hello?"

"Do you know where I live?"

It's Tommy. How did he get my number? "Yes." I don't bother lying.

"How do you know that?"

I followed you. I googled you. "I just do."

"Get over here. Now."

"Excuse me?" I don't take commands.

He doesn't respond and instead hangs up.

That pisses me off and has me driving straight to his place.

He knows I took his stuff. Otherwise why call me? But he's not stupid. Neither am I. Obviously, there's going to be a confrontation. A confrontation he's inviting. Fine by me. I'm not scared of him. Why should I be?

I knock. He opens. I step inside. He closes and *locks* the door. My stomach muscles contract at the click.

He grabs the front of my jacket and shoves me up against the wall. "Who the hell do you think you are?"

I narrow my eyes. "I *suggest* you release me."

Instead Tommy steps closer and I feel his breath on my face. "I ask myself, who would benefit from looking through my place, taking my laptop, my drives, my file of the *Decapitator*. Your name is the *only* one that comes to mind. The niece of the Decapitator. A girl, who at three, saw the first kill. A girl, who I'm positive, is still hiding more."

"Back. Off," I warn him, feeling equal parts guilty I took his stuff, cautious at his temper—albeit justified—and turned on at his roughness, his nearness.

"Where's my stuff?" he demands.

I bring my knee up so he can feel it against his balls. "You want me to follow through with this, I will."

Tommy doesn't move, and I inch my knee a fraction higher. Neither one of us speaks for a tense few seconds, and my mind reels with how to handle this. Finally I come up with, "I should've never *trusted* you with that information."

Throwing out the word "trust" hits its mark, and I can see his brain reanalyzing things.

I don't wait and forge on. "We had a deal. I told you something huge about myself, and you were supposed to tell me what you know about the Masked Savior following and M. You have yet to come through with your part."

"Because you're lying. You know it. I know it. Until I'm sure you're not lying, I'm not telling you shit."

"Lying, Tommy? Really?" I shove him away. "This is what you're going to hold over me? Please. My business is my business and that's all I have to say." I turn, unlock his door, and open it. "If you ever get rough with me again, you will most definitely regret it."

"Bring it," he challenges, and I shut the door right in his face.

As I charge back to my Jeep, all I can focus on is the rage surging through me. What is wrong with me? Why do I feel in control and at the same time misguided? Like I know what I'm supposed to do, yet I can't seem to make it happen. Like I'm grasping for something I can't quite get. No matter how much I deny it, I'm lost. And angry.

Angry at who I used to be and who I am now. Irritated I'm cleaning up my mom's legacy when all I want to do is forget it. Annoyed at how I handled things with Tommy. I mean, my God, at the base of it all he's just a guy grieving the loss of his sister.

Will it always be this way for me—this haze of confusion with clarity hovering just within reach? I just don't remember being this unfocused, this *emotional* before. I can't believe I just robbed somebody. I can't believe I've opened up to both Tommy and Dr. Issa. My God, I cried in front of Dr. Issa! I don't cry.

I climb into my Jeep and flip on the radio. ". . . Masked Savior has made personal contact," the reporter is saying.

I turn the volume up. The task force brought in some expert analyst to look at the letter I sent. Summary is: There is not one Masked Savior. The vigilante acts are being carried out by several different people who are being directed by one leader. It is projected the leader is an educated, forty-something, single woman with no children, who likely works out of her home.

Perfect. They are now officially off me and onto Marji. Payback.

Chapter Thirty-Two

DESPITE (OR MAYBE BECAUSE OF) HOW things went down with Tommy, I definitely go buy him a laptop and send it, along with the flash drive of his personal things, to his apartment.

IF I'M BUSTED, I WILL TELL THE COPS EVERYTHING.

This is a text I get as I'm coming out of the postal store. I don't know the number, but the area code is 804. Richmond. Marji. She's heard our local news and that makes me smile. Good, let her squirm. She's not going to tell the cops shit. She'd have to implicate herself in the decapitations, which would mean life imprisonment or the death sentence.

She's definitely bluffing.

I delete her message and don't bother texting her back. I won't let her think she's getting to me.

I go straight to Patch and Paw. I need some serious Corn Chip time. He is the one constant that not only helps me forget my crazy life but also allows me thinking time. I know that doesn't make sense—forgetting *and* thinking—but somehow it comes together in my mind.

He's not in his cage, and so I head out the side door.

Zach and Dr. Issa are in the yard laughing and playing with Corn Chip and several other dogs.

I stand for a second, undetected, just watching their excitement as they chase the dogs, throw balls, and laugh at each other and the barking. I can't recall a single time when I ever had that much carefree fun. There's got to be something wrong with that.

They both turn at once, as if sensing me, and both their smiles drop away.

Call me the Grim Reaper.

Or rather, Slim Reaper.

"I . . . didn't know you were coming in today," Dr. Issa ventures.

I look between them—the guy I had sex with and the brother who gave me a much-needed release. When did I become *that* girl? "I didn't know I was either."

No one says anything for a couple of seconds. Even the dogs fall silent.

"Did you want to play with us?" Zach asks at the same time Dr. Issa suggests, "Can you come back a little later?"

Wow. Okay. But . . . I get it. After what happened between us, Dr. Issa is uncomfortable around me and Zach. Plus they need their brother time. I just never thought Dr. Issa would be so bold in his statement.

"Yeah, see you around," I say, and head straight out, not even glancing back.

As I pull from the parking lot, I purposefully drive by the side yard where Zach and Dr. Issa and the dogs are all back in full play mode.

Yes, I would've liked to have played with them.

When I get home, Daisy and Victor are arguing, which is way too odd for me. Daisy and Mom, sure. Daisy and Victor, never.

"I don't understand what the big effing deal is," Daisy snaps.

"Watch your language," Victor warns.

"Lane gets to," Daisy snips back.

I immediately tune in. I get to what?

"Your sister is almost eighteen," he counters.

Daisy rolls her eyes—"Whatever"—and storms upstairs.

I get to what?

Victor sighs, defeated, and obviously at a loss. "I'm going

to the office." With that he's gone, and Justin and I exchange a look.

"What was that all about?" I whisper to my brother.

He gives me this look like, *Really?*

I shrug.

"Daisy wants her curfew upped, and she wants permission to go out every night like you do."

Oh. "But I only go to the coffee shop."

Justin rolls his eyes, mimicking Daisy. "Girls."

I laugh, and my cell buzzes. Catalina. "Hello?" I answer.

"You know that statement the Masked Savior sent to the press?"

I know it very well. "Yes."

"I just found out the task force thinks it's all made up."

Irritation flares in me and has me clenching my jaw. What did I do wrong? I thought that letter was pretty damn airtight.

I step out of the kitchen and into the living room, where my brother can't hear. "Why?"

"I'm not sure, but within the task force they're maintaining their original profile that there is a real Savior and then a copycat. Publicly, though, they'll stick with the one about the older woman. What was it exactly?"

Educated, forty-something, single woman with no children, who likely works out of her home. "I don't remember, but I know what you're talking about."

This is what I get for going on the offense. I work better in obscurity. I know this. I should've never sent that statement. They didn't even believe it. This is not good. "How do you know all this?"

She chuckles as if that's the most stupid question ever. "I bugged my dad's office."

Immediately I recall the nanny cam I planted in my mom's office. Seems as if Catalina and I share the same thought process.

"My dad's on the phone with your dad right now."

I glance down the hall to the office at the exact second the door opens, Victor steps out, and he looks right at me.

"Gotta go," I whisper to Catalina, and hang up.

Victor nods to his office. "We need to talk."

Chapter Thirty-Three

I READ PEOPLE WELL. VICTOR'S COMMANDING tone is enough to tell me I should channel my most respectful, polite self. "Yes?" I ask as I take a seat in his office.

He closes the door and takes a seat too. "Your Gramps was *convinced* you weren't doing what you said you do at night."

Excuses and responses begin to formulate.

"I checked up on you," he continues. "You weren't at the coffee shop last night."

That's right. I was breaking into Tommy's house. "Does this have anything to do with Daisy wanting an upped curfew?" I try to divert him.

Victor levels me with a very disciplinary stare, and I

immediately recognize I shouldn't have brought Daisy up. "Where were you?" he asks, instead of giving my question consideration.

"I went to Tommy's house. He's in my grief group." Now let's just hope Victor doesn't check with Tommy.

I expect this response to appeal to his understanding side, and even soften him, but instead he delivers one very FBI-affirmative nod.

I give him the most honest stare I can. "Actually, I visit a lot of places. Parks, grief group, coffee house, library—and sometimes I just drive around." Following people.

"The whole reason why your mom and I let you go out every night is to get away and study. Not to roam the streets."

This is not what I need right now and is exactly why I always have to stay one step ahead. I can never be unprepared.

"Yes, sir," I answer him, praying he doesn't put me on restriction. It's not often I respond with a respectful "sir," but it seems extremely appropriate that I do so right now.

He motions to the door. "You can go."

I head straight upstairs to find Daisy in my room.

"Will you talk to Dad for me?" she asks.

"Not going to happen. I sort of just got in trouble," I honestly tell her.

This brightens her mood. "You?"

"Listen, just lay low." I give her advice I've already given myself and haven't followed. "Be on your best behavior and let some time pass. I think Dad's just really overwhelmed between work and us and Gramps's visit and Mom. . . ."

"Well," Daisy sighs. "Now I feel like a bitch."

I smile. "Our family's going through a lot right now."

"Anyway," Daisy continues, "I came to apologize. I shouldn't have brought you up in making my point."

"It's okay."

"And I have a question. Hammond's invited me to his house for dinner. He's cooking and everything. Will you drop me off? He said he can bring me home."

"Sure."

"Just think, in a few months I'll have my license, and you'll never have to chauffeur me again."

There was a time when I looked forward to that too. Lately, though, driving her around hasn't bothered me so much.

"All right, I've got homework to finish." And with that she's gone.

I sit for a second at my desk, thinking back through the conversation with Victor. He's always trusted me. He's never questioned me before. Gramps must have really gotten to him.

I drop Daisy off at Hammond's, then go straight to my grief group meeting. I don't expect to see Tommy, and when he walks through the door late, I straighten in my chair. He doesn't glance at me one single time. Grief group lasts an hour or so, and when it comes to an end, he immediately leaves.

Why did he bother coming?

As I approach my Jeep, I see a note stuck under the wiper. It simply says:

I'm returning the laptop.

I crumble the note, shove it in my pocket, and climb into my Jeep. To hell with Tommy. He doesn't want a new laptop, then whatever.

After our conversation, I don't want Victor losing his trust in me, so I text him: DAISY DROPPED OFF. GRIEF GROUP OVER. AT PATCH AND PAW.

OKAY, he simply responds.

I drive around for a while, watching my rearview, trying to lure *anyone* out: Marji, j_d_l/copycat . . . Finally I head to Patch and Paw.

I let myself in the night door. Corn Chip isn't here, and so I grab a couple of kittens to play with. As I tickle their bellies, my thoughts drift to Marji, Mom, me. How could they hurt these poor defenseless little things? How could they make me? It's just sick. Wrong. And horrible.

Laying low or not, this weekend my focus is Marji. I'm done with her part of all this. If she is connected to the Masked Savior site, if she is by some chance M, then not only will I sever that tie but also the last link to the Decapitator.

If I'm busted, I will tell the cops everything. I don't intend on busting her. My intentions lie elsewhere.

"Hey."

I glance over my shoulder to Dr. Issa, standing a hesitant distance away.

"What are you doing here?" I ask. I didn't see his car in the lot.

"I've been here awhile. Had a couple of surgeries and was following up with notes." He glances at the kittens and smiles a little. "You really do have a way with animals."

This sends a pleasing calmness through me. "Thank you. I needed to hear that."

He gives me a curious look.

I tuck the kittens back in their condos and stand up. "Well, that's all I wanted. I'm out of here."

"Lane?"

I stop.

"I didn't mean to be rude to you the last time we saw each other." His brows come down. "I'm sorry."

I shrug it off. "I understood. You and Zach need time together. And you're uncomfortable being around me after what happened. I get that."

He chuckles. "Leave it to you to just lay it out there."

What does he expect?

Dr. Issa shuffles his feet, still a little uncomfortable. "Well, anyway, thanks."

I nod.

He jiggles his keys. "Let me just get my coat and I'll walk out with you."

We exit the night door and head around to the front, where I come to a frozen stop. Beside my Jeep is a dark blue BMW with Marji sitting inside.

My blood heats as I stare at her in what at first is surprise but slowly becomes anticipation. *This weekend, Marji, this weekend.*

Marji lowers her window. "Hello, Lane."

"I don't want to talk to you."

She cuts her gaze to Dr. Issa, then back to me. "You will eventually."

"No. I. Won't."

The corners of her lips curl up, and there's nothing sweet about the smile. She drags her eyes back to Dr. Issa and gives him a slow, creepy once-over. Then she rolls her window up and drives off.

I don't like that she looked at Dr. Issa. Mess with me and it's one thing. Screw with my friends, my family—hell, no.

"Um . . . ," he ventures. "Want to tell me what that's all about?"

No.

"You seemed surprised, and obviously not happy to see her. Is she—"

"She's nobody."

He grabs my arm and turns me to face him. "Who was she?"

I look into his understanding eyes. "*That* is my aunt."

It takes him a second to digest that. "Oh."

"I would appreciate it if you keep this to yourself. No one, and I repeat, *no one* knows about her. I'm actually still puzzled over the fact I told you. I need more time to process before I go to my dad." Of course I have no plans to go to Victor, but I know it makes sense to say so.

Dr. Issa releases my arm. "You can trust me."

"Trust." Such a simple word. I would like to be able to trust somebody. Completely. I just don't think it's possible with who I am. I've got to be okay with that loneliness. I just do.

I look over to my Jeep. "I should go."

"What does she want with you?"

To play. To tease. To taunt.

Dr. Issa steps into my line of sight. "Lane, let it go. You don't need to carry this. Focus on the future, not the past. Give this over to your dad to handle."

Oh, I'll focus on the future all right. Marji is the last connection to the Decapitator and my past. A connection that will be permanently cut.

"Focus on change." He continues his Dr. Phil advice.

Change? I'll never change. "I will," I appease him.

As I cross the parking lot I think back to when I visited

Marji in her townhome. How my blood boiled. My reckless driving back up I-95. Then jumping Dr. Issa.

I glance back and give him a once-over. He won't be my "out" this time. I'm channeling it all into Marji.

My pulse thumps. Just once. All through my body. Marji and my mom were sisters. I know exactly the evil I'm up against going after her.

Chapter Thirty-Four

ON FRIDAY EVENING I SAY, "DAD, CAN I GO
to the movies tonight?" It's the weekend so curfew's not until one.

"Who are you going with?"

"Myself."

"Tysons?"

"Yes."

"Okay, be back by one."

I give him a quick hug, not overdoing it, grab my things,
and head out.

Marji, here I come.

I hop on the interstate, and with every mile that I drive
south, eagerness, anticipation, and excitement builds in me. I
wonder if Marji can *feel* that I'm coming. I hope so. I want her

good and aware that *I'm* the one who is stopping her.

I know exactly what I'm going to do. I'll ask her to go for a drive. I know she will. She wants to play with me as much as I want to play with her. When we're out of the city, I'll find a secluded spot and lure her from the Jeep to go for a walk and "talk." I'll taser her, zip-tie her, and find out if she's M.

Then, after I do what I have planned, I'll just leave her in the woods. Whatever happens to her, happens to her. I'll take my ties and the Taser cartridge with me. I don't want any evidence linked to the Masked Savior.

If she doesn't get the hint to stay out of my and my family's life, then I'll come back. *I'm* the one making the threats tonight, not her. After tonight she'll realize the things I'm really capable of.

When I get into Richmond, I drive straight to her townhome. I park several blocks down and take a few seconds to methodically check all my supplies. Taser, zip ties, gloves, and my new addition—one very sharp butcher knife. It only seems fitting as she was intimately involved in the decapitations.

I close my eyes and breathe out, imagining the knife sliding across her skin. Every cell in my body twitches with just the thought.

I check everything one last time, grab the handle on my Jeep, and catch sight of a dark blue BMW coming from the opposite direction. I shrink back a little and watch as it passes by me and the entrance to Marji's townhome community, and then merges with traffic and takes the on-ramp north.

Well, damn. I wasn't expecting that.

I crank my Jeep, whip the wheel around, and gun my engine. I cut straight across three lanes, ignore the honks, and follow her onto the on-ramp.

I don't immediately see her BMW, and I whip around a semi, floor the gas, and keep heading north.

A couple miles up I finally catch sight of her.

She's driving in the fast lane, and I keep up. There's tons of traffic, it's dark, and with everyone's headlights I highly doubt she notices me.

Seconds tick into minutes tick into an hour and finally she exits and heads west.

Highway gives way to country, and eventually I shut my headlights off and follow as far behind as I can, with confidence she doesn't see me.

She takes a couple of switchback dirt roads and eventually comes to a stop at a run-down mobile home on a huge piece of empty, wooded land.

I tuck my Jeep in the woods and watch as she climbs out, grabs bags from her trunk, and heads inside the front door. A few lights go on, and I see her shadow as she moves through the trailer.

I'm not even going to wear my mask. I want her looking

right at me when I execute my game plan. Marji will know she is suffering for all those innocent people she participated in torturing and murdering.

In my secure spot I look around. Frozen trees. Snow. Bushes with twigs for limbs. From the sound, a river bubbles somewhere nearby. The last house I saw sat several miles back. Marji's out here alone. She's been playing me, taunting me. Is this a trap?

She comes back out the front of the mobile home, opens the back door of her car, tosses a blanket aside, and brings out a . . . *body*?

Oh no.

I squint my eyes. The body is slender, and I assume from the build that it is a young woman or possibly a teenager. I make out duct tape around the arms and legs and a hood over the head.

My heart speeds up as I watch Marji drag the body across the yard and into the mobile home. I cover my face with my hands. *Oh. My. God.*

Okay. Focus. Obviously, Marji is here to do something to this person. Likely torture and kill. Just like my mother and father had. Trying to carry on the Decapitator's legend or vision or whatever sick thing is going through her mind.

I shake my head. No. This can't be happening.

She's probably going to do the same thing that my parents

did. Strip the woman naked, strap her to a table, and slice her head and appendages right off.

I clench my jaw. This stops tonight.

I grab my binoculars and quickly take in the structure. I don't see outside security cameras anywhere, which doesn't surprise me. We're so far out in the country, nobody probably knows this place is here. There's got to be a back door. I'll head there.

I triple-check my supplies, pull my ski mask on because I don't want the captive to identify me, and climb from my Jeep.

I jog through the woods and come up on the rear and notice, as I'd hoped, there is a back door. Good. Carefully I approach it. Stop. Listen. Creepy merry-go-round music can be heard through the flimsy walls.

The back door swings inward, and Marji points a gun at me. I take a shocked step back.

She grins. "I *knew* you were following me!"

Her excitement brings a focus, a stillness over me that I welcome.

She rakes her disgusting gaze down my body. "*Love* the Masked Savior getup."

I don't respond, and my finger twitches on my Taser.

She motions me in with the gun. "I have a surprise. You get to sit and watch." She shrugs. "Or you can pitch in if you're so inclined."

My mom had wanted that. To do Zach together. *We'll go down in history as the most infamous serial killers never caught.*

I shove her voice from my head and concentrate on the here. The now. I play this creepy-ass plot the only way I can. I make nice. "Mom wanted that too."

Marji's smile fades, just a little.

I inhale a deep breath, and as I blow it out, I close my eyes. "I miss her, Marji. So very much. I didn't want to admit it at first, but you remind me of her." I open my eyes and show her sincerity I do not feel. "I haven't been able to stop thinking about you."

Marji's face gentles into a loving curve. It disgusts me.

I look down at the ground, humble, submissive. "That's why I followed you tonight. I was hoping we could talk"—I lift my face—"or something. You're the only person who under-stands me."

She tilts her head—"Oh, Lane"—and lowers the gun.

I jerk my Taser straight up and shoot. Marji's gun clanks to the floor. She lets out a high-pitched wail as the barbs pierce her skin and she falls forward from the back door. I jump back to give her twitching room in the dirt.

I slide the butcher knife from its case, and with two hands I bring it straight up . . . a quick flash of my Mom doing this exact same thing goes through my brain.

I give my head a shake, grip the knife even tighter, and

stop. Wait, what am I doing? This wasn't part of my plan. I was going to torture her, not kill her.

If I kill her, I'll become my parents. This echoes through my head, and I give it another shake.

Marji twitches a few last times, and then her body slowly calms. She focuses on me through the cold darkness and lets out an evil giggle that ricochets through the night. "You can't do it, can you?"

My grip tightens.

"I'll kill you," she sneers. "I'll go after Victor and Daisy and I'll save Justin for the very end. I'll peel the skin right off of him, just like I did those cats. Just like I did that other little boy last year."

Other little boy?

She grits her teeth and pries one of the Taser barbs from her stomach. I give it a quick glance to see it glistening with blood and torn skin.

"Oh, you didn't know about that. Little Gary Streeter." She lets out another evil laugh. "I burned his body right on this property. No one even knew."

Why is she taunting me? Does she *want* to die?

"Just like no one will know about Justin."

Rage surges through me, boiling my blood. My grip tightens even more, sure and steady, and I let out a deep scream as I plunge the knife straight down into her chest.

Skin gives. Muscle tears. Bone crunches. Blood spews. I draw in a sharp breath. My heart hammers in my chest cavity as I stare down into Marji's wide, cloudy eyes as life rushes from her soul. My entire body flashes hot, then goes ice cold. Bile rises, and I swallow it down.

My gaze goes to my two hands, twitching on the handle.

I fall back on the ground and scoot away from her body, gasping now for breath.

I just killed her. Oh my God. I just killed her!

I swallow again and focus on some deep breaths in followed by slow exhalations out.

Time passes, I have no clue how much, but my heart gradually slows to a controllable pulse.

I want to do it again reverberates around in my head. I want to feel that blade going into her body. The crushing bone. The tearing muscle. The coppery scent of blood. Yes. Again.

I reach for the handle. And freeze.

No. Stop. This craving. This desire to do it again. Like a drug. An addiction. I can't. I won't. This is what drew my mom, my real dad, Marji into the darkness. I can't let it have me, too.

This is not my fault.

I'll peel the skin right off of him.

Oh God . . . I stumble away, tear the mask off my head, and dry heave.

Carnival music slowly filters into my consciousness, and

I jerk straight up. The person inside! Shit, I forgot about her!

I tug my mask back down, step over Marji's body, and head inside the mobile home.

I catch quick glimpses of candles, hanging straps, and chains. What was Marji going to do?

I find the iPod docking station and turn the music off.

More candles flicker from a back room, and I follow their glow to find a cage with the woman inside. She's still unconscious with a hood and duct-taped limbs. Other than that she doesn't appear to be harmed, and I can tell from her rising and falling chest that she's breathing.

I try to pick the lock on the cage and can't.

I look around for a phone, find Marji's purse back out in the kitchen, and dig around inside.

I get her cell out, and stop.

I should look around first, before I call for help, see if there's anything in here linking my parents to Marji.

I open every cabinet, every drawer, every anything I can find. For the most part the place is empty. Just some canned tuna and bottled water. And of course her torturing devices. This would be the place to keep something, though. Not at her townhome.

I take Marji's cell back to the cage to see the woman starting to stir. An old-fashioned jewelry box catches my attention, and I lift the lid to see it crammed with pictures. I thumb through them in disgust. They were taken right here in this room as she held captive and tortured a little boy who I assume is Gary Streeter. Others are of a teenage girl put through the same cruelty. The rest are of Marji and my parents.

I take the ones of my parents, dial 911, put the phone down, and get the hell out of the place. As I step from the trailer, Marji's lifeless body draws my focus, and I walk over to it. I no longer feel sick or panicky; now it's pure repulsion.

What a heartless bitch.

As I sprint to my Jeep, I hear the woman inside scream. The complete terror in her voice makes my gut clench, and I ignore my instinct to want to go back and help her.

Emergency services will be here soon.

When I'm back on the highway, I pull over and wait. Eventually sirens blare in the distance, and I watch as one cop, then two, then several more, and then an ambulance turn onto the dirt road.

I take the first true breath that I've had since arriving at that hell.

Marji will *never* hurt anyone again.

But I didn't find out if she's M or even linked to the site and the copycat.

Chapter Thirty-Five

I ARRIVE HOME A LITTLE AFTER CURFEW AND quietly ascend the stairs. Victor peeks his head out of his bedroom, gives me a quick survey, and says, "You're ten minutes late."

I do *not* feel like dealing with this right now, but I draw on every patient fiber I can find in me. "I apologize. Traffic." Traffic is always a good excuse in this area.

If Mom were still alive, this wouldn't even *be* an issue. Hell, if Mom were still alive, I would've never found out about Marji. I wouldn't have just *killed* her sister.

An image of me puncturing Marji's chest flashes through my brain, and I flinch. God damn.

"Lane?"

I blink. "Yeah?"

"What's wrong?"

"Not a good night," I honestly tell him.

His face gentles with concern. "Need to talk?"

"No." Yes. No. I stare at him a second, my mind reeling. What would he do if he found out about me? He'd be disgusted. He would *not* understand. I'm not entirely sure why, but my gramps pops into my mind, and I ask, "Why doesn't Gramps like me?"

Victor studies me for a couple of long seconds like he's trying to formulate his response. "It's not so much that he doesn't like you, it's more about your mother. He never did warm to her. In all fairness, she never liked him as well. Your gramps didn't want me to marry her, and he was very vocal about it."

So Gramps picked up on her creepiness when no one else did. "Do I remind him of Mom?"

"You do. But you should take that as a compliment, Lane. Your mother was a respected and loved woman."

I nod, even though I don't take it as a compliment at all. "So I've never specifically done anything to cause Gramps not to like me?"

Victor takes a few seconds again, and I get the impression he's not going to tell me the truth.

"Please don't hide anything from me," I implore. "I can take it."

He sighs. "When you were really young, he caught you on several occasions pulling legs off spiders, burning ticks, and doing various other things with insects. You also found a dead squirrel, dissected it, and put it in a jar. It worried him."

I change my mind. I don't want to hear this. I thought I did, but I don't. I don't want to know I tortured any innocent thing. I don't want to know I kept dead animals in jars.

"Lane." Victor's voice softens to match his expression. "It's perfectly natural for kids to go through stages. That's all it was. A stage. Look how wonderful and caring you've become."

I nod, because I know that's what he needs to see, but I in no way feel wonderful and caring. I grant him a tiny smile, ready to just go to bed. "Good night, Dad."

"Good night."

He closes his door, and I stand in the hall for a moment, thinking. Tortured insects. Tortured cats. Animals in jars. I wonder if that's all. God, I hope so.

Shame, guilt, and repulsiveness have me closing my eyes against memories I can't seem to recall. I'm fitting those serial-killer profiles more and more each day, and unfortunately, I don't think there's any stopping it. Which is why I have to channel it in the right direction. It's my only hope at not going insane.

I head to my bedroom, step inside, and immediately sense someone's been here.

My gaze darts from my bed to my closet, my desk, the

window, then over to the dresser. I go straight there and open the underwear drawer.

My box is gone.

Shit.

Victor . . . *No* . . . I go back across the hall to his room, raise my hand to knock, and stop. Wait. When was the last time I saw the box? Two days ago. That excludes Gramps. Unless Gramps told Victor about it, and then he went into my room to see. . . .

No, I don't think so. If Gramps had told Victor, he would've ratted me out publicly.

I change directions and tiptoe downstairs straight to the office. I look through every drawer and cabinet not locked and find nothing. I head down to the basement and open our storage closet. I rifle through, come up empty, turn, and freeze.

"What are you doing?" Daisy asks.

"Why are you up?" I counter.

"Thirsty. Saw the basement light on."

I shut the storage door. "Were you here tonight?"

"Yes. Hammond came over for a while."

"You didn't go in my room, did you?"

"No."

"Justin? Dad?"

Daisy shakes her head. "Not that I know of. Why, what's going on?"

"Nothing. Go back to bed." I push past her and race back up the stairs.

In my room I look out the window, and sure enough my fire-escape ladder is unhooked and hanging down the side of the house.

Son of a bitch. Someone broke into my room.

Chapter Thirty-Six

THE NEXT MORNING VICTOR TAKES DAISY to Saturday cheer practice, and Justin plunks down in front of the TV. I use the time to double-check my family for my missing box. I search through Daisy's room, Justin's, Victor's, and come up with nothing.

I go to my Saturday Patch and Paw shift, burn the pictures I found at Marji's trailer and go through the motions of working, but I'm completely preoccupied.

I would naturally think Marji had taken my box, but there's no way she could've broken into my room and been with me at the same time. However, Tommy . . . of course. I break into his place, so he retaliates by breaking into mine.

I sigh. This isn't good.

I finish off my shift and drive straight to his basement apartment. I knock, he opens, and I step right inside.

He doesn't back up. "Let me guess. You're missing a box."

"Who do you think you are, breaking into my room?"

He smirks. "Ah, the irony."

I narrow my eyes. "I want my things."

"I would like mine. But here we are."

"I bought you a new laptop."

Tommy's smirk gets even bigger. "Look there. You finally admit it."

I close my eyes and draw in a deep breath because my blood is seriously starting to roil.

He snickers and my eyes snap open. "Give. Me. The. Box."

He takes an intimidating step toward me, all smirks and snickers gone. "Can't. I disposed of it. What are you going to do about it?"

I shove him hard in the chest; he stumbles away and comes right back at me. I hike my chin, showing him I'm *anything* but intimidated, and he puts his face right in mine.

"Get out," he commands.

He's seen my journals. My dark side. My obsession. *He has to die.*

My whole body goes numb.

He has to die? What am I doing?

I broke into his place. He retaliated by breaking in to mine.

Tommy's a victim. His sister's a victim. We're all a victim of my mother.

He doesn't deserve to die. He doesn't deserve any of this.

"You come here in control. Then when I challenge you, you get angry. I give the anger back and you freak. Now you're panicked." His voice calms. "That's a lot of emotion in the span of a few minutes."

How is he so intuitive? How is it he sees so much when everyone else sees nothing in me?

I turn away, ashamed, humiliated. This isn't me. I don't taunt and go after innocent people. Everything Tommy's done is out of retribution for his sister.

My journals: Sure there were clippings, notes, details, but nothing personal. Nothing incriminating. All done from an analytical point of view. In reality Tommy hasn't discovered anything other than that I research, follow, and collect serial killers through time.

This. Me. Us. It's wrong. I shouldn't be here. I freaked on him for nothing.

"You need to leave," he quietly says.

I don't turn and look at him. I simply nod and walk from his apartment. I don't want people knowing I'm mesmerized by killers. I just don't. I'm not ready to share that part of me with anybody.

Reggie's the only person who knows that side of me, and she only knows a small amount.

As I drive home, all I can think about is what just went down with Tommy. *He has to die.* What the hell am I thinking? That's something my mom would have thought. Or Marji. Or Seth, my real dad. I don't think that way. Not about someone like Tommy.

When I get home, I go to our backyard and look up at my window that I always leave cracked for fresh air. It's easy enough to release the ladder. Even a long tree branch can unsnap it. But how did Tommy know that window was mine? My eyes narrow in on the present Justin gave me last year—a stained-glass "LANE" suctioned to the window. Of course.

All my years of research, details, methodical notes. It's gone. It's all gone.

I close my eyes. *Tommy* . . . There'd been a connection there, initially, through the grief group. He'd taken me for a ride on his bike and helped me feel free. Then the link between his sister and the Decapitator came to light. Followed by finding out he was part of the Masked Savior following. Then my sharing one of my deepest secrets with him.

How did I go from feeling free around him to breaking into his home? It's all frustrating and puzzling, and somewhere deep down I want things to go back to the way they were, but I'm not sure how to reverse them. This is exactly what happens when emotions get involved and confuse things.

I trudge inside, and I crank my laptop up. The last time

I looked, there had been no report on Marji or that young woman. Surely, there's something now.

I scroll through my news feed and sure enough, there it is:

RICHMOND LOCAL MARJOREAM VEGA FOUND STABBED

Quickly I peruse the article. The young woman in the cage was eighteen. Marji picked her up outside a bar. The young woman thought they were going somewhere to party.

Yeah, Marji's kind of sick party.

The article talks about little Gary Streeter, who has been missing a year, and the person in the other pictures, now identified as a sixteen-year-old girl who has been missing for five years. At least the families can have some sort of closure.

My mother is not mentioned once. The fact that they are sisters is hidden deep. Just like everything else in the Decapitator's life.

The article goes on to speculate as to who stabbed Marji. To my surprise the Masked Savior isn't even mentioned. Probably because a knife was used and no zip ties, and it took place outside of Richmond, not here. Though there was a Taser. Whatever the reason, it's a blessing. For sure.

I read the rest, where they report the knife used to stab

Marji is missing. They combed the surrounding area, but couldn't find it.

My heart picks up its pace as I reread that part. *Missing?* No. I left it there. It shouldn't be missing!

I press my fingers into my eyes. This can't be happening. My copycat, j_d_l, was there. He, or she, saw the whole thing.

Chapter Thirty-Seven

I CAN'T SLEEP AND AM UP BEFORE FIVE MAK-
ing coffee. Sometime between reading the news about Marji
and realizing my copycat saw it all, I convinced myself to take
a day and just exist. Think things through, regroup, and come
up with my next steps.

Plus, I need to spend time with my family. Because who the
hell knows how this is all going to play out.

I want to practice aikido with Justin, challenge Victor to a
game of chess, and *definitely* have some sister time with Daisy.
I want to feel things out and see if she's hiding anything from
me. I want to make sure she knows I'm here for her.

The three of them are all I have now.

I make a spread: frittata (Victor's favorite), chocolate-chip pancakes (Justin's), and blueberry muffins (Daisy's).

Victor wakes up first and comes downstairs in his pajamas. "Lane? What are you doing?"

I motion to the oven, where the food waits on warm. "I made breakfast." I give him the rundown. "Everyone's favorite."

His mouth quirks into a pleased, if not perplexed, smile. "Wow. Um, thanks. What's the occasion?"

I shrug. I'm not one for touchy-feely statements, but I hope my actions show.

He gives me a hug and kisses the top of my head. "That's really sweet."

"I was thinking you and I could maybe play chess later?"

His brows come down, accentuating his already perplexed smile. "Okay, but Justin and I have a nine a.m. tee time, and then we're doing a late lunch/early dinner with some of his aikido pals."

"Oh . . ."

Victor gives me another hug. "I'm so sorry."

"That's okay," I mumble. Really, what was I expecting? To suddenly want family time and they'd be at my call?

"But let's definitely all do breakfast." He rallies my brother and sister out of bed, and we all sit down to the feast I've made.

"Lane, I think you should be a chef," Daisy comments, and I smile.

"You know what I miss? Mom's bacon," Justin says, and we

all agree. She did make some great bacon. And though Victor's tried duplicating, there was just something about Mom's.

The rest of breakfast is lighthearted and easy—the way it should be. At least on their end it is. On my end, though I don't want it to, my brain wanders. . . . How can I sit here eating breakfast with them as if I didn't kill Marji? As if I didn't slice our Mom's head off? What if they found out? Would they still love me? Probably not. They'd be horrified. No matter how justified my two kills were.

Afterward Victor and Justin leave, and I find Daisy in her room, talking on FaceTime with Hammond.

She glances up from her iPhone to where I stand in her door. "What's up?"

"Thought we might hang out?" I awkwardly suggest.

She gives me the same perplexed smile Victor had. "Who are you and what have you done with my sister?"

I don't like that Hammond can hear this.

She waves the phone in the air. "Hammond and I are spending the day together. I already cleared it with Dad."

"Oh, okay." I back out of her room. Hopefully, she and I can talk tonight.

I wander into my room, pick up my phone, and dial the only other person I consider family. Reggie. I want to apologize again and just talk. She's right. It's been too long. One ring. Two. Three. Four. Voice mail. With a sigh I hang up.

Reggie's freezing me out and that just sucks. I've always had Reggie.

But somewhere in the back of my mind I knew she and I would probably part ways. Maybe Catalina's entrance into my life is some sort of sign. My next phase in the friendship thing. Masked Savior following aside, I could see that. She and I connect on a different level.

I look at my dresser and think of my journals. I do want them back. I get in my Jeep and drive straight to Whole Foods where Tommy works. I'll talk to him. Try to reason with him. This is what I think as I cruise the parking lot and identify his motorcycle, but right as I'm about to park, I change my mind and pull back out. He's not going to give them to me. If I want them, I'll have to take them back.

As I drive to his apartment, I glance in my rearview more than once. I don't see any suspicious cars following me. Whoever is trailing me is good. To have followed me to Marji's and watched, and I had no clue. Yeah, they're good. *Too* good.

I go to Tommy's apartment, park on the street, get my lock-pick tools out, and stop. *Jesus.* Here I am again. At Tommy's. About to break in and get my journals back. He has to know I would do this. Of course he wouldn't keep them in his apartment.

Plus, what am I doing?

Didn't I convince myself just last night that this thing

between Tommy and me had gotten out of control? That it has to stop?

I can't spend the rest of my life cleaning up the Decapitator's mess, hiding facts about myself and my family, and running from my past. It has to come to an end sometime.

Doesn't it?

A rumbling engine catches my attention, and I glance in my rearview mirror to see Tommy coming down the street. *Great.* He pulls right past me and into the small parking lot. He throws his kickstand down, kills the engine, and climbs off.

He walks to his door, turns, folds his arms over his chest, and just stares at me.

Waiting. Waiting for I'm not sure what.

I'm wearing shades. He's wearing shades. We can't see each other's eyes. But as the seconds, then minutes tick by, I get the distinct impression our staring match shares mutual thought.

"This has got to stop," he calls out, putting words to my exact feelings.

I nod. I know. But I'm not ready to talk about it right now. I consider asking him to take me for a ride on his bike, if anything so I can lose myself in the speed and the wind. But I don't. I don't want the rejection of him saying no.

Instead I crank my engine and drive away. Maybe in a few days I'll be ready.

When I get home, Daisy and Hammond are making out

on the couch. Hammond leaps off her like I shot him with my Taser. "S-s-sorry!"

I've caught her having sex, so this, my friend, is nothing. Hell, you're both still fully clothed. This is what I want to say, but of course don't.

Hammond grabs up his stuff and fumbles/stutters/rushes his way out the door with a "See you tomorrow" mumble to Daisy and one last guilty "Sorry" to me.

When he's gone, I look at my sister, and we both can't help it—we laugh.

"I think *I* just fell in love with him." I make a rare joke, and my sister laughs even harder.

She straightens her clothes. "How about movie and popcorn?"

I smile. That sounds good. That sounds *more* than good. I don't want to make anything awkward, so I'll talk to Daisy tomorrow. Feel her out. See if she wants to talk about anything.

As the movie's beginning, Victor and Justin get home. My brother plunks down beside me on the couch, Victor stretches out in one of the oversize chairs, and we all have the family time I woke up this morning wanting. Needing.

I savor every second. I'll tell however many lies I have to in order to keep things just like this.

Chapter Thirty-Eight

THE NEXT MORNING AS I'M WALKING INTO school, Catalina calls me. "I finally had that phone call with the leader. With M."

I wave Daisy on and walk a few paces away. *"And?"*

"Oh, God, it was the most exciting, inspiring fifteen minutes of my life."

"Inspiring." She'd used that word before when talking about the Masked Savior's vigilante acts. "Is the leader a man or woman?" I ask, praying she says woman. Please let Marji have been M.

"I don't know. The voice was disguised."

I inhale a not-so-patient breath. "What did *he* or *she* want?"

"I'm not allowed to say anything." Although I can't see her, I can tell she's cringing. "I'm sorry."

My teeth clench. "When did you have this phone call?" Please say a time before I killed Marji.

"Last night."

Shit. Which means Marji's not M. "And you can't tell me what the phone call was about?"

"I can't. I'm sorry."

"Well, why call me?" I snap.

Silence.

I tune in to the pulse thumping in my neck. I'm done with these games.

"*Don't* get that way with me," Catalina warns.

I narrow my eyes. I've never heard that tone in her voice before.

"You need to apologize," she says.

"Yeah, that's not going to happen."

She clicks off.

I shove my phone in my pocket and head inside school. Reggie's mad at me. Catalina's mad at me. Fine. What was I thinking, trying to have friends?

As I pass by the administrative suite, I see several policemen and women gathered in the office, and I come to a complete stop.

What the hell is going on?

"What do you think that's all about?" Kyle whispers from my side.

I shake my head. Are they here for me? Did the person who took the knife come forward with details? Heat flashes across my skin. It can't be.

The bell rings, and I don't move. Kyle tugs me toward homeroom, giving me an odd look. Stiffly I follow him, and five minutes in, our principal announces we're on lockdown. My entire body tenses, nerves twitch, and every muscle in me clenches. Are they going to barge in here and handcuff me?

Dogs are brought in to sniff lockers. What are they looking for—don't dogs sniff for drugs? What do drugs have to do with the Masked Savior and me killing Marji?

Either way, there's nothing in my locker but books.

My Jeep.

Oh no. My Taser is there. My zip ties. The tranquilizer gun. My ski mask. My cargo pants. It's all there in a bag hidden in the back.

What was I thinking? I need to ditch all my supplies. There can be nothing tracing me to the Masked Savior.

I flick my eyes to the clock. When will they lift lockdown?

Homeroom comes and goes, and ten minutes into first period the principal announces we can switch classes.

I fight every urge to run and instead make my way to my TA job in the library. Rumors zip through the halls: drugs, weapons, and on and on, but I block them all out. Somehow I need to get out to my Jeep and ditch my kit.

I go straight to Mr. Bealles, the librarian. "I know students are not allowed off campus, but I left my calc homework at home. I can go home and be back before the bell rings."

He gives me a long study. I've never once asked for anything in this place and I've never been in trouble, so I highly doubt he'll suspect an ulterior motive.

"Fine," he gruffs, reaching into his pocket. He pulls out a pass and quickly scribbles his initials on it. "I will not excuse you if you're late coming back."

I take the pass and hurry out to my Jeep. I gun it out of the parking lot and race several blocks over to an apartment community. I grab my kit, wipe it down of fingerprints, and throw it in a Dumpster.

I make it back to campus with five minutes to spare and race across the parking lot. Right as I'm reaching for the door, I stop.

The tiny hairs on my arms lift and a creepy shiver tenses my neck. Someone's watching me. I turn and stare out across the sea of student cars all the way to the road—at least a hundred yards away—and in the shade of a tree stands a person. Man or woman I'm not sure. But in the shadows they seem more tall than short. More skinny than fat. More dark than light.

It reminds me of the night outside of grief group when I saw a person standing on the street.

The person turns and seemingly disappears into the shadows, and my heart pumps a few extra times. That's no coincidence. That's my copycat. That's the person who saw me stab Marji.

I go about the rest of my day. I sit through my classes. I don't hear a word, though, from teachers, from students. All I can think about is that person. Who is it? Who the hell is following me?

When the final bell rings, I race out to my Jeep. While I wait on Daisy, I get a closer look at that tree and the shadows. Behind it stretches a path that leads through a neighborhood and into a park.

Daisy approaches. "Hey, what are you looking at?"

I climb in my Jeep. "Nothing. Let's go."

As we pull from student parking, I see Zach standing off to the side talking to Kyle. Seeing the two of them together strikes me as odd. They both catch sight of my Jeep and give me simultaneous polite smiles.

Daisy waves. "I didn't know they were friends."

Me neither. That's one more thing I have to worry about now. I don't like Kyle talking to Zach.

We pick Justin up and head straight home. As we walk in the door, there stands Victor, and Catalina's father—the head of the task force—with Catalina right beside him.

"Justin, Daisy, go to your rooms," Victor says. He motions

the rest of us into the living room. "Let's all sit down."

I chance a quick look at Catalina to gauge what the hell is going on, but she's purposefully avoiding my gaze. Probably because of our little disagreement earlier. My thoughts spiral with why they are both here, but I force myself to stay calm. Focused.

"Last night," Catalina's father begins, "there were several incidents in the area. *Tragic* incidents. Eyewitness reports and evidence point to the Masked Savior as responsible."

"What incidents?" Catalina interrupts.

"I'm not at liberty to go into details." He looks between us. "I understand the lure of this thing. Righting a wrong. Taking justice into your own hands. I know both of you have been active members on the site."

"I've only made a few posts," Catalina says, conveniently leaving out the fact she's the administrator and that she's had a phone call with M.

I would leave that out too.

Her dad looks at me. "And you?"

"I had an account and I took it down," I tell him.

"Most of the people seem harmless, Dad, really." Catalina looks at me. "Wouldn't you agree?"

I nod, because really, what am I supposed to say?

"They discuss mostly what the Masked Savior did." Catalina laughs. "Someone even posted a brownie recipe once. Except one time there was a string about darkest desires. . . ." She looks right at me. "Did you happen to read that string? It was creepy."

"Yes, I did see a few of those. It was creepy," I agree, and think about Kyle.

"Well, we've been monitoring the site and we know exactly what's getting posted. The members do seem young," he tells us. "Some things we read prompted us to do a sweep of all the high schools today."

Now that I think about it, with the profile, I'm surprised they hadn't done that sooner.

"Did you find anything?" Catalina asks.

"Again, not at liberty to say. But I wanted to meet with you girls personally. First, I don't want either one of you on that site again. Second, if you hear *anything* around school or your friends, you need to tell one of us"—he nods at Victor—"immediately. Okay?"

Catalina nods.

"Yes," I say.

Victor sees them out, and after he closes the door, he turns to me. "Is there anything you're not telling me?"

"No, sir. I'm not hiding anything."

Chapter Thirty-Nine

THE NEXT MORNING I KNOCK ON DAISY'S door. "Can we talk?"

"Sure." She waves me in.

I close her door and sit down at her desk. I've never known how to do the pleasantry part of a conversation. I always get right to the point. But as I stare at her sitting on her bed, I spin a few niceties through my brain, trying to come up with exactly what I want to say.

She laughs. "Lane?"

I chuckle too. I really don't know how to ask her if she has any dark thoughts or urges without it coming across odd.

So I decide on, "Ever since Mom died I've been remembering a lot of things." *Like the Barbies and the meat mallet.* "Kind of like you remembered your eighth birthday." *And Marji's name.*

Daisy nods.

"I guess I just want you to know that you can come to me if you remember things and have questions. Or if you have any thoughts you want to talk about. You will never get judgment from me. Only support and honesty." I study her eyes, trying to show her in mine how serious I am.

To my surprise she doesn't do a typical giggle-it-off Daisy move. She nods thoughtfully.

"No matter how odd the memory seems," I clarify. "Okay?"

Daisy's brows come together. "Like what kind of odd memories?"

Why is she asking me that? Has she had one? "Anything," I assure her. "No matter how off it seems, and I'll help piece it together." Or I'll help bury it. "Like the name you overheard—Marji. I found out she was just some friend of Mom's from when they were kids."

"Why were Mom and Dad arguing about her?"

"Because"—I decide to tell her the truth—"Dad didn't really like Marji." I shrug. "Just like you and I don't like people."

This seems to appease her, and she smiles. "Did you learn all this big-sister communication in your grief group?"

I hold my hands up—"Busted"—and we both laugh. "I guess that's enough bonding for now," I joke, and get up.

"Thanks, Lane," she says as I head out.

"Sure."

The conversation was a good start. Not too deep. Not too light. Just enough to lay the foundation for follow-up. Enough to let her know I'm here if she wants to talk. I don't want her to be confused or lost like I've been with my thoughts, my impulses, my needs.

All I can do is keep an eye on her. Be here for her, and hope she wasn't exposed to the same things I was as a child. Hope we're not doomed to be the evil mirrors of our mother and Marji.

I research the incidents Catalina's father mentioned—another prostitute and another homeless person attacked. Suspected drugs are involved with both. All done with Tasers and zip ties to copycat me, and beaten afterward. No deaths. Just beaten. Horribly beaten with a baseball bat.

Catalina said the task force thinks there's a real Savior and a copycat. I wonder which one they think did these. I wonder if Catalina knows.

After my Wednesday Patch and Paw shift I climb into my Jeep to go home, and catch sight of Dr. Issa sitting over to the side on a bench beneath a parking lot lamp. He's talking on the phone and hasn't even seen me come out of the building. It's not often I get to sit and just watch him.

I crack my window and his voice floats in, but I can't make out what he's saying.

Memories of the first time I met him come back. I was fifteen and had just started working at Patch and Paw. He came in as an intern, straight from Hopkins. He introduced himself, we shook hands, he gave me that shy, intelligent smile, and my heart experienced its very first female flutter.

I smile a little to myself.

Done eavesdropping, I go to roll my window up and see him stand.

He paces away from the bench and back, his voice lowering in anger. He stops talking, listens, then fires back a retort. He brings the phone away, looks at it, and puts it back to his ear. "Hello?" I hear him say, then he chucks his phone into the bushes.

He kicks the bench, and it reminds me of the time I saw him kick his tire after an argument with a girl.

Dr. Issa's temper always catches me off guard. I've seen it flare a few times, but it just seems so . . . not him.

He retrieves his phone and heads inside, and I continue sitting for a few minutes. What gets him so angry? A girl? His father? I wouldn't think Zach.

I check my watch. It's a little after nine. Catalina's house is on my way home, and so I do a drive-by. If she's home, I'll stop and see where she and I are in things. See if she's still pissed at me for snapping at her.

See if she's learned anything from her dad's bugged office.

Her VW Bug is not outside. I pull along the curb and parallel park among all the vehicles in her neighborhood. I'll wait a few minutes and see if she shows up. There are a few lights on downstairs and one on upstairs. But her room is dark.

I turn my Jeep off, and while I wait, I start to think through things. There are three people I know for sure are or were members of "my" site: Kyle, Catalina, and Tommy. There's j_d_l, who, from the posts, I'm positive has been following me. Then there's M, the creator of "my" site. Finally, there's my copycat, who I've been convinced is j_d_l. But what if he's not? What if M is my copycat?

Either way, the two people I know for sure with a direct link to M are Catalina and Tommy. I've already searched Tommy's place and came up with nothing. I look up to Catalina's dark window. It's time I searched her.

The ancient VW Bug putters in from a side street and hangs a left into her driveway. She doesn't even notice my Jeep parked along the curb in between all the other vehicles. Still, I duck down in my seat and watch as she gets out. She grabs a duffel bag from her backseat, pops the lock on her front trunk, and stows it inside.

She heads into her house, and I stare at her car. I bet anything if she has something I want to see, it will probably be in her car, not her bedroom. Just like me—I keep stuff I don't want people to see in my Jeep. Like my Masked Savior kit.

I don't have time to look now. But later tonight . . . well, that's a different story.

I glance at my bedside clock, watching as it transitions to two a.m. It's time. Dressed in all black with my long hair shoved up inside a dark beanie, I stealthily climb down my fire escape ladder and hit the ground running. It's sprinkling, but not full-on rain yet.

I jump in my Jeep and drive straight to Catalina's house. I park a couple blocks down and look around. I am the only one out.

I speed-walk my way to her Bug, which she's moved from her driveway to the curb to make room for another car. Probably belonging to one of her parents.

Her Bug is old with no security. It should be easy to break in to.

I peer into the front, the back. It's clean. No garbage. No anything.

Way back when I was little kid, Victor drove a VW Bug. That's how I know the engine's in the back, storage is in the front, and the hood release is located in the glove compartment. I also recall watching Victor wedge his fingers in the wing window and pulling up on the door lock.

I mimic my memory, wiggling my hand through the side window and down to the lock.

I open the door, pop the glove compartment, release the hood, and round the car to the front.

Inside the storage area there's a duffel bag. I quickly rifle through it and find a change of clothes and toiletries. I set the duffel aside, and in the darkness I feel around. Wires. Tubing. A tank of some sort. All on top of a piece of plywood.

With my gloved fingers I find the corner of the plywood and lift up to discover a small lockbox hidden beneath. It reminds me of the one my parents keep passports and birth certificates in. Why would Catalina have something like this?

I lift it out, put everything back like I found it, and speed-walk back to my Jeep.

It takes a deviant to know a deviant.

That thought enters my mind and makes me pause. Me and Catalina. Deviants. Deviating from the norm. Yes, that would describe us.

In my Jeep I get my pick and work the lock. I can't get it to open. I press the pick a little harder and it snaps off. *Damn.*

In the early-morning darkness I squint but can't really see the broken piece in the lock. I don't want to turn on a light. So I put my Jeep in gear and drive home. I'll get some of Victor's tools and jimmy it open.

Back at my house I climb up my ladder and slip into my room. I open my door at the exact second Victor's light flicks on.

Shit.

I yank my beanie off and dive for my bed and under the covers and hope to all holy hell I look like I'm sleeping.

He opens my sister's door first . . . then Justin's . . . then mine.

The lockbox. I put it beside my bed. I don't think he'll see it. It's dark in here. Or did I? Oh my God. Where *did* I put it? I didn't leave it by the window, did I? This isn't like me. Hasty. Scatterbrained.

Leaving my door slightly open, Victor turns and shuffles back to his room. I listen for his door to close, but it doesn't. A few minutes later I turn in my bed and look all the way down the hall to his cracked door and the light spilling out.

He's up. Either he can't sleep or he's going into work early or both. Either way, him being up means I'm going nowhere. I can't go down to the basement where he keeps his tools.

The lockbox. I glance over the side of my bed, locate it, and slide it under. I lie back, stare up at the ceiling, and think about the box. Down on my floor. Calling me. Taunting me. Luring me to open it.

Chapter Forty

IT RAINS HARD THE REST OF THE EARLY
morning hours. I don't sleep and finally get up at five, my usual
time. I'm exhausted.

The lockbox is still under my bed. Victor's downstairs now.
There's no way I can go to the basement and get his tools without him knowing. Asking.

I do the only thing I can do: grab a shower and head downstairs.

"You look tired." He points out the obvious.

"You too." He's been up the same amount of time as me.

"Couldn't sleep."

I nod and refill his mug.

Victor takes it. "I'll be in the office."

As soon as he closes his door, I race down to the basement, dig around in his toolbox, and get what I think I need. I head straight up to my room, lock myself in, and grab Catalina's box. I take a quick glance at my clock. We don't leave for school until seven. I have plenty of time.

It takes me a flat-head screwdriver and needle-nose pliers to get the broken piece out of the lock. With a new pick I gingerly work it, and in a few minutes I hear a *click*.

I breathe a sigh of relief. *Finally.*

I wedge open the lid.

A cell phone sits right on top, and I take it out first. Underneath are photos, newspaper articles, handwritten notes. Everything neatly clipped in organized piles.

I lay it all out on my bed, and it's like looking at my own collection and research of serial killers throughout time.

I scan through her notes, and even though they are her personal thoughts, they're done in a scientific, third-person point of view. Much like how I do mine. Chronicling the killer's childhood, nature versus nurture, leading up to his or her killing spree.

I continue unclipping and scanning the bundles, each with a family tree of sorts attached. Catalina tracked the family members of the serial killers and what came of them. I've never thought to do that before.

I read through her notes, fascinated at the slight trends she's identified. Parents of killers, siblings, extended relatives, children of killers . . . I track my eyes down those paragraphs: isolation, lying, stealing, violence . . .

Yes, I am my parents' daughter. I've come to terms with that. It's how I channel it that is the key to me not turning into the evil that was them.

DECAPITATOR peeks out from under a separate bundle, and apprehension buzzes through my blood. The newness of the bundle and fresh-dated notes indicate this is her latest research project. She's compiled a file much like I had, following the Decapitator's every move. There's a printout of my mom's funeral; another of Zach, the one surviving victim; and one of me, the only known relative—the Decapitator's niece.

My picture's attached to a small spiral notebook. I open it and start reading. Dates. Times. Places. Details of the cheerleader's head I shaved. Graffiti boy. Jacks, the druggie I almost took down but didn't. Aisha. The locker at the Metro stop. Marji . . .

Son of a bitch! Catalina's the one who has been trailing me. *She's* j_d_l!

There's a knock on my door. "Just a minute!" I shove everything back into the lockbox and slide it under my bed. I give my room one last look and open my door.

Catalina's standing there with Victor behind her. I stare straight into her face. j_d_l. She knows everything about me. She saw me *kill* Marji! Her dad is the head of the task force. Why hasn't she turned me in? More important, how did she manipulate

253

me, how did she *lie* to me all this time and I had no clue?

She's j_d_l, but is she also my copycat?

"She has a question for you," Victor tells me. "I told her to make it quick. You're getting ready for school."

I wait for him to leave, but he doesn't.

She grins. "Hey, there's some stuff missing out of my car, and I was just wondering if maybe you accidentally took it the last time we were hanging out?"

I don't break composure. "No." How in the hell does she know that?

She cocks her head. "Oh, okay. Well, if you find my stuff, just return it whenever you're ready."

What kind of game is she playing here? "Okay."

She waves. "Have a good day."

I watch as Victor walks her down our stairs, and I hear her go out the front door.

Catalina is my dark mirror. That's what I thought when I first saw her. We *are* disturbingly similar. Save for one very valid point: I don't have frontal lobe issues and she does.

She does things and doesn't think they're wrong.

Victor's words nudge into my brain and have me pausing and questioning not Catalina, but my own self.

I didn't intend on killing Marji. It just happened. Did it surprise me? Yes. Did it make me sick to my stomach? Yes. Do I currently feel remorse? No. She threatened me, my family. She participated in the Decapitator's mutilations, and she tortured two people (that I know of) all on her own.

She does things and doesn't think they're wrong.

The fact is, I *could* have killed other people, but I haven't. I would *never* hurt somebody who didn't absolutely deserve it. Never. I know the difference between right and wrong. If it can't be honestly justified, then I don't justify it.

What am I doing—the last thing I need is to question myself. I need to get back to compartmentalizing. I used to do it so well. The ability to execute my initiative, flip the internal switch, and go back to being just Lane.

I've lost that part of me.

Before Mom, Catalina would never have been able to manipulate me the way she has. No more struggling with thoughts and actions. It's past time I get back to being me.

In first period library TA, I turn on the phone I found in Catalina's lockbox and scroll through the numbers. I'm in there. So is Tommy. Kyle also. A few other names I don't recognize. There's one number she's called the most. There's no name attached to it. Just a number.

I type it into a couple of different search engines and come up with nothing. It's probably a burner phone.

"Hey, you."

I glance up. "Zach. Hey." Talk about forever.

He smiles, and the absolute honesty in it softens my heart,

and it hits me—Marji, Catalina, my mother—it seems I'm des-
tined to be surrounded by unbalanced people. How am I so
fortunate to have someone true like Zach?

"I miss you," he boldly states. "*Really* miss you. I thought I
could do this stay-away-from-Lane thing, but I can't. I'm sorry to
keep going back and forth with you like this." He heaves a sigh that
turns into a desperate sort of confused look. "I'm saying I want to
be friends again. I *need* to be your friend." He swallows. "Please."

I smile as his words wash over me. "Definitely friends."

He blows out a relieved breath (like he really thought I
would say no). "Want to do coffee or something?"

"Sure."

"Okay, I'll call you." He gives me a quick hug and bolts back
across the library.

That was . . . strange. And pretty damn great.

I close down my station and grab my stuff. Catalina's phone
vibrates. I glance down at it, surprised, and stare at the mystery
number listed on the screen. This is the perfect opportunity for
me to find out more, impersonate Catalina, do a little digging
of my own, unearth *her* secrets.

I grab the phone and slide it open.

DID U DO IT? the mystery number texts.

I type back, YES.

I wait. And wait. And wait some more. But the mystery
number on Catalina's phone doesn't respond.

Did I do what . . . ?

I'll bet anything the mystery number belongs to M. It's my turn to manipulate things. I've got to figure out how to meet this M and deal with Catalina.

Although I'm not quite sure what "deal with Catalina" means. She knows too much. My God, she knows I stabbed Marji. I just wish I knew how deep Catalina is with this whole Masked Savior copycat thing.

Now that I know she's been watching me, I need to backtrack and think things through. She knows who I am—obviously. She probably started following me because I'm related to the Decapitator. Then she merely stumbled across the fact I'm also the Masked Savior.

She's known all along who I am. She's been luring me into her friendship. She's been feeding me information about what the task force does and doesn't know.

She knows I have her lockbox. Which means she knows that *I know* what she has been up to.

The question is, why do all this?

And how dangerous of a threat is she?

There's no telling how much she's lied to me about. For all I know she and M could be one and the same, but I'm just not seeing it. My gut tells me they are two different people, which means one of them *has* to be the copycat.

Unless there's a third person involved. . . .

Chapter Forty-One

THAT NIGHT VICTOR GETS HOME LATE, AND I'm on the couch watching TV. "Hey," I tell him.

He blinks tiredly and looks around. "Daisy and Justin are in bed?"

"Yes."

"What'd you guys do for dinner?"

"Breakfast."

He gives me an exhausted smile. "That sounds good." He slides in beside me on the couch, lays his head back, and closes his eyes. I take in his frown lines, the gray that seems to be more prevalent now, and his stubble. He looks ten years older than he did just a few months ago.

There're so many questions I want to ask him. Like why

did he marry Mom, was he happy with her, did he ever pick up on anything different about her, did he suspect anything about Marji, and did he know Daisy's not his?

But of course none of these questions come out.

"What are you doing down here all alone?" he asks on a yawn.

"Thinking," I honestly tell him.

"About?"

"You and Mom," I venture.

Victor opens his bloodshot eyes, and the tenderness in them has me sliding over and laying my head on his chest, just like I used to do when I was younger. I inhale the faint scent of familiar cologne, and it comforts me.

"Why did you marry Mom?" I quietly ask.

"Well, for one, I fell in love with an adorable red-haired toddler." He tugs my hair and I smile. "But your mom was . . . fascinating. She was so driven and strong and unlike any other woman I had dated. Honestly, she got pregnant with Daisy and that's what nudged us both into marriage." He gives my shoulder a gentle squeeze. "Best decision I ever made."

How dare my mom lie to him about so many things. She knew Daisy was Seth's and yet moved forward with marrying Victor. Moved forward with having a "normal" life. She knew Seth couldn't give her what she wanted. What a manipulative bitch.

Victor strokes my hair as if sensing my tension, and it feels so good, so loving, so gentle, and it calms me back down. "I hope you know I never once thought of you as Seth's. You're mine. Plain and simple," he tells me.

"Thanks," I whisper.

A few quiet minutes go by, and I listen to his heartbeat as I get lulled by the sensation of my head rising and falling with his breaths.

"I love all of you kids. More than anything."

He didn't say he loved Mom.

Zach sits with me with at lunch. "So how's little man?"

I smile. "He's good."

"Daisy and Hammond seem the couple." He nods across the cafeteria to where my sister sits giggling and snuggling with her boyfriend.

"Hammond's good for her," I say, using Daisy's terminology. It's people like him who will keep her normal.

Zach cuts his brown eyes over to me. "*You're* good for her."

Hmm. No one's ever told me that before.

"You're good for *me*, too," he stresses.

I roll my eyes in a very un-Lane-like way. "Please. You're making me blush."

Zach laughs at that. I like that I can make him laugh.

We continue eating in silence for a few seconds, chewing, looking around.

"You notice anything going on with my brother?" he asks.

"No. Why?" Other than our mutual orgasm and the temper flare he doesn't know I witnessed.

Zach shrugs. "I don't know. He seems so in and out. You know?"

"No, actually I don't know."

"It's like one minute he's the best brother in the world and the next I can barely find him. I just . . . Sometimes I wish the clock could rewind."

"Yeah, that I do know."

We keep eating, and my thoughts drift to Dr. Issa and the few heart-to-heart talks we've had. "Know that he's trying, Zach. Losing a parent is not easy."

"I hate that you know that."

No one's quite put it that way before. But how true that is.

Zach wipes his mouth and stands. "Nice to be friends again. See you around."

"Yep." I watch him weave his way through the cafeteria, and glance over to Daisy again. She's looking back at me with a little smile that I return.

She turns to leave, and Kyle is standing behind her, propped against the wall and staring right at me. My smile slides away as I take in his perplexing gaze.

Inside my backpack Catalina's phone vibrates, and I glance

away to dig it out. When I look back up, Kyle is gone. What was *that* about?

I slide the phone open, see it's from the mystery number, read 2000 FORD CIRCLE, FAIRFAX. SAT. 9PM, and my stomach muscles clench in anticipation. Finally!

Saturday at nine. I'll be there, and I'll be ready.

Chapter Forty-Two

I DECIDE TO GO TO AN EXTRA GRIEF GROUP meeting, thinking Tommy might show. He doesn't, and I find myself completely preoccupied by that one single fact.

How is he?

Maybe I should go to his apartment and just . . . see.

As I'm fitting my key into my Jeep door to go home, I sense more than see someone behind me. I turn. It's Catalina. She grins. Why is she always so happy?

"What do you want?" I ask.

"To say hi," she says.

I don't respond.

"So, I've been thinking about something, and I knew you could appreciate it."

I still don't respond, but I do wait. How is she going to broach the subject of j_d_l and the Masked Savior?

"My life has really been one big tragic mistake. I could be such a different person right now if certain things hadn't happened when I was younger."

Not what I expected her to say. By "certain things" I assume she means the accident that caused her brain damage.

"Even though you probably won't admit it, I think the same holds true for you."

She's right about that.

Catalina pauses, glances out through the night, and then finally brings her gray eyes back to mine.

"The thing is," she goes on, "I think you and I could be the best of friends if we wanted. Yin and yang and all that. We're more alike than you think. Yet so very different. There's something unique about you, and I'm extremely intrigued to find out what caused it. Will you tell me?"

"No," I finally speak.

She cocks her head. "Despite what you think, I'm not the bad guy. I have no plans to give the police my records."

There it is. Verbally out in the open. Her admittance of what we both know. "You don't have any records," I remind her.

She smiles. "That's right. *You* have them. That took balls, by the way—"

"I don't have balls."

"—and honestly if it had been anybody else, I would've already retaliated. The fact that I haven't is a show of respect."

She needs to get to the point. "I don't want your respect."

She finally moves and takes a step closer to me, but it's not a threatening closeness. It's more of a comforting closeness. "Lane, it's okay. I admire you. I would never do anything to mess with who you are."

I take a deep, bored breath in and exhale loudly through my nose. "Yeah, and here's my thing. I have a little thing called cognitive processing and impulsivity restraint. Which I under-stand some of us don't."

Her brows lift. "Ouch. I guess I deserved that."

I almost smile at the unexpected idea that comes out next. "I'm seriously considering going to the cops. Just turning myself in. Coming clean."

I haven't been, of course. But saying the words is oddly . . . liberating. Peaceful even.

Catalina shakes her head. "You don't want to do that."

As long as we're having this little heart-to-heart . . . "So where'd you get j_d_l from?"

She shrugs. "Justin-Daisy-Lane."

I'm sure she thinks she's incredibly clever with that one. "So are you going to go ahead and tell me you're M, too, and my copycat?"

She chuckles. "Sadly, I'm only j_d_l. I really have no clue who M is or the copycat."

I curl my fingers into my palm so I don't throw a punch, and glance at my watch, making it more than obvious I'm both done and tired with this conversation.

She reaches for me. "I know you're mad at me for lying to you. I promise to keep your secret. Please don't worry. I accept you fully for who you are. There's no judgment from me."

I just look at her.

She sighs. "You need to come to terms with who you are, Lane."

Her gentle voice makes my teeth start to clench, and I concentrate on not showing her a reaction.

She doesn't move as I turn, unlock my Jeep, and climb inside. She still doesn't move as I crank my engine, put it in first, and drive off. And she still doesn't move as I turn the corner out of sight.

Right now if I could get rid of Catalina, I would. This is where *not* having a conscience would be a fabulous thing. I could merely end her life, dispose of her body, and call it a day. Then there would be no witness to the things I've done.

Sadly, I'm only j_d_l. I really have no clue who M is or the copycat.

She sounded sincere. She looked sincere. But she's done nothing but lie to me. How can I believe her now?

I promise to keep your secret.

I can trail her, sure. But with her already following me, it's the proverbial cat-and-mouse chase.

Yeah, ending her life would be an obvious solution, and that thought just pisses me off. I've had more lack-of-conscience contemplations in the past few months than I have ever.

I am my parents' daughter. I know this. But there is a fine line between good and evil that separates us. I will not cross it. I will not harm an innocent person.

I accept you fully for who you are.

I hate even more how great that sounds. When did I ever need that kind of acceptance and validation?

As I'm pulling up to my house, my cell rings. It's Tommy. What do you know?

"Hey, Tommy," I greet him, like there's been nothing awkward between us.

He chuckles at my tone and it makes me smile. I like his chuckle. It's deep.

"Listen, my bike's broken down on the parkway straight across from Georgetown University. Can you come get me?"

I'm glad he's called me. "Does this mean we're friends again?"

"It means I need a ride."

Tit for tat. "Be there in a bit." I text Victor and he texts back, YOU'RE A GOOD FRIEND. BE HOME BY MIDNIGHT.

I head off, definitely anticipating, not dreading, seeing Tommy. I'm not sure what to think about that. Why did he call me?

Dr. Issa, Zach, Tommy. It seems I'm surrounded by those who have lost people close to them. But then again I suppose grief attracts grief. We all "get" each other.

Just like disturbed attracts disturbed. Mom, Marji, my real father . . . me.

The parkway at night is beautiful. All twinkling house lights, the Potomac rolling peacefully, and the road gradually flowing with curves. It's not often I pause to think about those visually stimulating things. I should do it more often. It's . . . nice.

I see Tommy along the side, propped on his bike, just staring off at the same scenery I've been admiring. My stomach dances a little bit, and for a change I don't push the female reactions away. I just enjoy it.

They're what a typical girl would feel when looking at a hot guy. It's nice to be typical, if only for a second in time.

He climbs into my Jeep with his book bag. "Hey, thanks for this. Triple A's going to tow it."

"Sure." I pull out, and we ride a few minutes in silence. "So why me?"

Tommy sighs. "I wanted some alone time with you."

"Oh?"

"You stole my computer and all my Decapitator research. Why?"

"I was scared," I honestly tell him. "That's my past and it hurts and I don't want people dredging it up."

Tommy nods. "I was wrong to do so. Things got out of hand between me and you."

"They did," I agree, so happy he's putting words to my previous thoughts. "I apologize. Will you keep that new laptop now?"

"Yes." He unzips his backpack and pulls out my journals. "I'm sorry for breaking into your room and taking these. I was trying to retaliate and hurt you in return. Except . . . this shit's creepy."

Creepy. He's right; it is. I hate that he knows this part of me.

"Will you tell me about them?" he asks.

I glance over at my journals. They both lighten and darken my heart. I'm glad to see them, but they're a reminder of who I really am. "Thank you for not destroying them."

Tommy nods and places them on my backseat, and as he does, I catch the scent of leather just like before. "You know, Lane, it's good to have one person you can be one hundred percent honest with. A person you don't have to lie to. A person you can trust."

This is sounding a little too uncomfortably like the conversation I just had with Catalina. Plus . . . I lie to everyone. I can't imagine not. "Are you saying I'm lying?"

"I'm saying you haven't been completely honest with anyone probably ever. Except right now. I sense an honesty between us that's probably new to you."

Hearing him say that gives me courage. "Have *you* always been honest?"

He chuckles, and it resonates deeply in the small space of my Jeep. "Of course not. But I do want someone I can be my absolute self with. Someone I'm not scared around."

I think about the similar words Catalina said, and the thing is, that *would* bring me a sense of rightness too. Complete acceptance by someone for who I truly am. Someone who wouldn't manipulate me for their own desires. "Are you saying you want me to be that person for you?"

"I'm not sure yet. But I do know it's got to be a two-way street. All I'm asking is that you think about it. And let me know your thoughts, okay?"

"Okay."

Tommy reaches forward to turn my heater down, and his fingers brush mine, which are resting on the stick shift. "Mind?"

I shake my head and glance down at his hand as he pulls it back. He has a new tattoo spreading out over the top of his hand and disappearing up under his leather jacket. "What's up with all the tats?"

He smiles a little. "My sister. She was an artist. I've been getting parts of her paintings put on me. My way to remember her."

"That's a great way to remember someone." Makes perfect sense, actually. "I'd love to see your arms sometime."

"Okay." He glances back to the journals. "Now that I've shared a chunk of me, will you tell me about those?"

I don't immediately. He reaches over, gently puts his hand on top of mine, and gives it a warm squeeze.

I want to turn my hand over and link fingers with him, but I don't.

His phone rings, and he slides his hand away to look at it. Whoever's name he sees makes him sigh, and he hits ignore before shoving it into his back pocket.

"Everything okay?" I venture.

A muscle flexes in his jaw. "Fine."

Some edgy seconds go by as he turns to stare out his window, and with each one the space between us grows.

I want the closeness back so I say, "Serial killers intrigue me. Just like they intrigued my mother. Perhaps it's because my mom hunted them that it took hold in me, too."

He turns to look at me. "Do you think you want to make it your life's work like your mom did?"

"No," I answer. "I don't want to be anything like my mother."

Chapter Forty-Three

AS I PICK MY WAY THROUGH CAFETERIA SPA-ghetti, my conversations with Catalina and Tommy are all I can think about. Catalina thinks she and I can be best friends, and Tommy wants a partner to come clean to.

Why, though, are they both coming to me? I exude anything *but* self-help.

However, Tommy's words do have an appeal. It would be refreshing to have one person to connect with, to share all my obscurity, and to know it comes with no judgment, only acceptance.

"Judgment." That's the word Catalina used.

I look across the cafeteria to Zach at the salad line and then over to Daisy sitting beside Hammond.

Zach and I have made a connection for sure. But somehow when I play things out in my mind, I don't see him handling my dark side. Although he'd hide it well—I don't see him walking away, but I do see him being repulsed. I'm sure he would urge me to "get help." And he would constantly check in on me to make sure I'm "okay."

It would be annoying.

Then there's Daisy, who six months ago I would've never even contemplated but now find myself pondering. I think my sister's hiding something, even if she doesn't know what yet. Me opening up to her would perhaps unveil her own hidden desires that I most certainly don't want surfaced. But me *not* talking to her might lead her down a path that she keeps hidden from me.

At this point I just need to watch her. Be there for her. Point her in positive, light directions. And hope beyond all hope she keeps buried whatever might be simmering in her.

Zach sits down across from me. "You look even more deep in thought than usual."

I take in his too-healthy salad and curl my lip. "I'd give anything to see you eat a big juicy double-decker."

He laughs. "I want to puke just hearing that."

We both go back to eating, and a few seconds later Zach speaks. "I told my brother you and I are friends again."

"Oh?"

"He was happy for me. For us."

I nod, even though I'm not entirely sure I like Dr. Issa and Zach discussing me.

Zach shoves a mouthful of salad in. "He also cautioned me to take it slow. That you're not a typical girl."

Not a typical girl? Well, he is right about that, but I do need to make things clear. "Zach, I love being your friend, but you know that's all we can be right now, right? Friends?" I can't be anything else.

Zach laughs. "I know, Lane. Don't worry. I'm not going to confess my undying love for you."

I laugh too, feeling just a little stupid. "Okay."

On Saturday I go to my Patch and Paw shift. I grab Corn Chip and a few others and head outside for a much-needed play session. But I'm completely preoccupied with tonight. Nine p.m., 2000 Ford Circle. It can go so many different ways.

My copycat might be there ready to take someone down.

Or my copycat could be there waiting for me.

Or M might be there expecting to meet with my copycat and gets me instead.

Either way I'm going to be early, scope things out. Wait. And I'm taking a weapon I've used for years in aikido and know better than anything—a bokken. As a wooden practice sword, it's not sharp, but it's deadly if used correctly.

I needed something new. I needed *me*. I'm not tranquilizer and knives. I'm aikido studied and trained. That is how I will bring my victims down. *That* is me. *You need to come to terms with who you are.*

Catalina said that to me. What she doesn't realize is that I have.

"Lane?"

I turn to see Dr. Issa stepping outside. I give Corn Chip a good rub and throw the ball. He scrambles away.

"Heard you and my brother are *friends* again."

Nothing like getting right to the point. "Yes."

"It's interesting; I go back and forth with you."

"Meaning?"

"When I first met you, I was intrigued by you. Not in a weird way," he quickly clarifies. "You were fifteen and so quiet and extremely intelligent and focused. I've never met anyone quite like you."

He's said as much before.

"There's something about you I can't figure out. You've got an old soul, and I truly believe you have the best of intentions. But—"

"Why are you saying all this to me?"

He pauses. "See—and that right there. You don't like a lot of conversation. You've always been a blunt girl. You are the epitome of black-and-white. Right and wrong. You're not afraid to just say it as it is. You're very unique. But . . . I'm not sure I'm comfortable with you and Zach being friends."

My heart pauses a beat. Am I that awful?

Dr. Issa shifts a little, making it obvious he's uncomfortable with this conversation. "The thing is, Zach is about the sweetest kid I know, and he has so many feelings for you. I don't think you realize that."

I turn to fully face him. "Are you saying I'm not sweet? That I'm not good enough to be Zach's friend?"

"I don't know what you are. But in the long run, no, I'm beginning to think you won't be the right thing for Zach."

Tears unexpectedly press my eyes, and I force them to stay dry. His words hurt, but I won't let him see it. "You feel that way, then you tell Zach. I won't." With that I walk off.

"Lane?" he calls.

"Go to hell."

I don't avoid Dr. Issa the rest of the day. In fact, I get right in his way. Let *him* be uncomfortable with what he said. I'm not.

Although . . . I really am.

I thought Dr. Issa and I had a connection, if only a little one; it *was* there. I'm sure of it. Maybe he's ashamed of what he and I did, and he's lashing out at me. Or maybe he's seen something in me that he previously didn't, and it scares him.

Either way, I'm not avoiding Zach. We're friends again. I *need* his friendship.

I sign out of work and head straight to my Jeep. It's six o'clock. I have three hours before I meet whoever I'm supposed to meet at 2000 Ford Circle.

I slip my key into my lock and immediately recognize my door is already open. I never forget to lock my door. Someone's been in my Jeep.

I search the front, the back, under the seats, the glove compartment. I go around the rear and open it. Just my aikido duffel, as usual.

I pick the carpet up, and right beneath, snuggled in its usual spot, is my old kit. The one I threw away. Complete with Taser, zip ties, cargo pants, ski mask, and tranquilizer gun.

Son of a bitch. Not only did someone see me throw this away, but they retrieved it, kept it, and have now planted it back in my Jeep for some reason.

To mess with my head or to play a joke or to frame me . . .

That's laughable. Framing me for basically being me.

I look around but don't see signs of anybody. Catalina's admittedly been following me, but after my run-in with her, I'm still not sure what I think about her. What I am sure of is that this is the work of my copycat or M. At this point they are the only two who would want to mess with me.

I truck it back into Patch and Paw and to the cremation room. I crank up the furnace and throw everything in. In the back under the ashes I see a chunk of Tommy's charred laptop that I must have missed. On my next shift I'll empty this thing out and clean it.

Yes, my copycat and/or M is definitely going down. Tonight. One way or another it's going to happen.

I still have hours, and I've already done recon via Google maps, but I drive on over to 2000 Ford Circle and scope things out in person. It's a deserted convenience store. Boarded up. Graffiti. Kind of out in the middle of nowhere. Not a bad part of town, or a good one, just out there. Works for me.

I drive around in circles, crossing neighborhoods, all the while keeping an eye on my rearview. I don't see any cars trailing me.

At eight p.m. I park a half mile down the road and get myself together. I slip into my new cargo pants and long-sleeve tee, bigger than the old ones and meant to mask how skinny I am. My new ski mask is lighter, made of neoprene, and easier to breathe through. I slide my bokken into its strap along my bare back and down inside my shirt, hiding it from view. The new zip ties and pepper spray I bought I tuck into my cargo pockets.

I wedge my fingers into my gloves, climb from the Jeep, and jog the half mile to the abandoned convenience store. Slipping the ski mask down over my head, I find a spot in the shadows behind an empty Dumpster and wait.

A dog barks. A chilly breeze flows past. One car zooms by. Still I wait.

8:45. Nothing. Not even the dog barking.

8:55. Still nothing.

9:05. A car pulls in, sits idle for a few seconds, and then the dome light goes on. It's a couple, and they're looking at their GPS.

Seconds later they turn around and head back the other way.

9:15. Nothing. Maybe this was all a hoax. Or whoever sent the text realized it went to the wrong person and aborted whatever meet-up they had.

9:25. Nothing. Five more minutes and I'll—

A prick stings my side. I jump and whip around, see another ski mask. And then my whole world goes blurry to black.

Chapter Forty-Four

MY EYELIDS SLOWLY LIFT. MY BRAIN GOES from knocked out to gradual conscious alertness. My head hurts. But not like I've-been-hit hurt, more like drug hurt.

I'm sitting on a metal chair with my wrists zip-tied behind me and to the chair.

I run my tongue around my mouth, work up a little bit of saliva, and swallow. I'm thirsty. How long have I been here?

I look around. Dark. Dusty. Empty metal shelves. A counter. An old cash register. I'm inside the deserted convenience store.

I crane my neck, look at the watch on my left wrist, and read 10:46 in the faint Indiglo. I've been out a little over an hour.

My heart kicks in with delayed nerves, fear, anxiety. I resist my natural urge to call out *Help!* and instead close my eyes, center myself, and concentrate on calm breaths.

It does me no good to be freaked right now. To resist the restraint. I need to channel balance, wisdom, stability, and alertness.

I tune in to my hearing and make out . . . silence. Whoever brought me in here is gone now.

I turn my head as far to the right as I can . . . and then the left. More dark, dust, and empty metal shelves. The only light in the place comes from one single bulb hanging above the counter and register.

In that second I see them, lined up on the counter: a Taser, zip ties, a tranq gun, my bokken, the knife I stabbed Marji with, and something I've never used—a baseball bat.

The others—they'd been beaten with a bat.

Every muscle in my body tightens. Are they going to torture me with these things?

I yank at the zip ties . . . and cringe. I yank some more— God, they hurt—and the slickness tells me I've cut my skin.

How long are they going to make me stay here tied to this chair? I could topple it over, but what good will that do? Then I'd be down on the dirty floor waiting for whoever is supposed to come.

I throw my body weight up, hoping to hop the chair, but the weight of it teeters me right back down.

My curfew is at one a.m. Maybe Victor will realize I'm not home and come out looking for me. But then, how would he find me? I didn't tell him where I was going. How would I explain this? *Dad . . . I don't even know where to start.*

I tug at my wrists, gritting against the slivering pain, and feel my left zip tie give way just a little. My nostrils flare on a scent of new blood. I wish I knew how to pop my thumb out of joint and slide my hand free. I try and grit my teeth even more. Ow!

The back door opens then, sending in a shot of fresh winter air and a quick flash of moonlight, and spiking my pulse.

"I've got her," someone says. "The one who has been beating up all those innocent people."

The door closes and I straighten. There's no way I'll show fear.

Catalina walks from the back door, looks straight at me, and grins. *Grins.* I narrow my eyes and I give her a quick once-over. She's dressed exactly like me. No deviation at all.

The person behind her steps into view and—

"Lane?" Dr. Issa says.

I feel my eyes go wide as I look from Catalina to Dr. Issa. What the . . . ?

He shakes his head. "Wait a minute. *You?*"

Catalina nods over to the counter. "Lane had all those things on her when I found her."

"You're a liar." I finally find my voice.

Catalina honestly looks offended. "Oh, I think we all know who the real liar here is." She looks over to Dr. Issa. "She doesn't get what we're doing. All we wanted to do was bring the drug dealers to justice, and she took off on her own. Beating innocent people. I've been following her for a while. I knew she had to be stopped. But I didn't want to call the cops until I could talk about it with you, M."

Dr. Issa just stares at me.

I don't speak. I don't think I can. Dr. Issa is M?

Dr. Issa?

"Michael." I use his name for the first time ever. "She is lying to you. Can't you see that? How long have you known me? How long have you known *her*? Do you really think me capable of beating innocent people?"

He shakes his head. "I don't understand. How are you even involved?"

"Because it's me. I started all this. Your website is *my* fan club."

"You're saying *you're* the Masked Savior?"

"Yes, but I don't touch innocent people. Ever."

"Well, we didn't either," Catalina interrupts, "until you came along."

I don't take my eyes off Dr. Issa, "Michael, she is lying to you. She's the one branching out on her own and copycatting me."

"Drug dealers," Dr. Issa clarifies. "Those are the only people I wanted to target." He paces away. "This has all spiraled out of control. I should've never gotten other people involved."

Catalina slowly moves toward the counter, and I watch her as I say to Dr. Issa, "Why *did* you start all this?"

"Because I wanted to avenge my mother's death. I wanted to tackle the drug problem that the cops can't seem to get a handle on. Then I met a few other like-minded people, and when the Masked Savior, *you*, popped onto the scene, it all seemed to make sense. Vigilante justice. Christ! But now . . ."

"Avenge your mother's death? I thought she died of cancer."

"No," Dr. Issa croaks, grabbing his head. "No. No. No. She overdosed. Our father wanted us to tell everyone it was cancer."

My heart breaks. "Michael, I'm so sorry."

"Oh, you guys are driving me nuts," Catalina spits.

Dr. Issa brings his confused eyes to hers. "*You?* You're the one who's been doing all those horrible things?"

Catalina rolls her eyes. "Don't take it personal. At first I was completely down with the vigilante thing and cleaning the streets of drugs. But then I realized there are also hookers and homeless people. . . . That's a lot to clean up."

Dr. Issa points at me. "Why is Lane tied up?" he demands. "What are you going to do to her?" He takes a panicked step forward. "Catalina, untie her. Now."

She snorts, "Yeah, like that's going to happen. See the thing is, I'm ready to take over this whole operation." She picks the Taser up and shoots.

"No!" I scream.

Dr. Issa drops to the dirty floor.

"Stop it!" I holler at her.

She presses the trigger again, and Dr. Issa arches off the ground with a howl.

I tug at my restraints. "Stop it!"

She drops the Taser, grabs the knife, and stalks over to him. "Ever since I saw what you did to that woman, I can't stop thinking about it."

My heart stops. "Catalina. No. Please. What are you doing? Stop!"

She rolls Dr. Issa onto his back and raises the knife high above her head. "I've never actually killed anybody."

"Doonn't . . . ," Dr. Issa slurs right as Catalina plunges the knife straight down into his chest.

Chapter Forty-Five

12:01. TEARS STREAM DOWN MY FACE AS I stare at Dr. Issa's lifeless, bloody form. Catalina stabbed him four more times. She counted . . .

One. Again in the chest.

Two. In the stomach.

Three. The leg.

Four. In the neck. Where she left the knife sticking out.

Of Dr. Issa . . .

This is all my fault. All of it. Dr. Issa, Catalina, all those people beaten to near death. My actions developed a following that twisted into this horrific ending.

The room closes in on me. My chest tightens. I'm in a darker place now than the night I killed my mother.

"Why so sad?" Catalina pouts. "You can admit that was thrilling to watch." She throws her head back and laughs. "Oh. My. *God* that was great! So much better than beating people with a bat."

It is my destiny to be surrounded by deranged people. It is not a destiny I want. But nonetheless it is mine. I stare at Catalina in disgust. Misery and craziness have found each other in her.

When did she become this person? Did she get so turned on by all the beatings and the empowerment it gave her that something flipped inside her, or was she this way all along and merely waiting for the time to develop?

Moods, impulsivity, behavior. It's all very clear now.

"So, what?" I ask. "I'm next?"

She brings her eyes down to mine. "Actually, I didn't plan any of this. M already told me he was done. That he didn't want anything to do with all the violence. I was going to set you up to take the fall. But, well, now he's dead. So I guess you'll take the fall for that, too."

Catalina walks back over to the counter, and I watch her as I use the few seconds to work at my slick wrists a little more.

She picks up my bokken. "This is new. What kind of damage did you think you'd do with this?"

Why don't I show you?

She slaps the bokken against her palm. "Way I figure, there's law and then there's life." She sweeps her hand over toward Dr. Issa. "He was trying to balance the two when really you have to pick one."

I pick life. My life. Not Catalina's.

I concentrate on no more tears. No more weakness. Only focus, and more important, revenge. "So let me get this right. You met Dr. Issa through the Masked Savior site. You said you wanted to 'fight crime' when really you just wanted to beat people up. You encouraged people like Kyle and Michael Mason to do the same. You posed as M, the leader, and Dr. Issa had no idea. At the same time you're following me, playing me, going behind my back, *lying* to me. Sound about right?"

She flashes me a grin that I used to think made her look happy, but now I clearly see the malice in it. "Yep, I pretty much lied to you about everything."

I twist my wrists a little more. "You're something else."

"Thanks."

"Brilliant, in fact." God, I hate her.

Her grin gets bigger. "Thanks."

I turn, and even though I don't want to, I make myself look at Dr. Issa. My throat swells, and I concentrate on not swallowing, on *not* showing my emotion. "You're right. I *did* enjoy watching that." I tell her what I know she wants to hear.

"I know, right?"

I tear my gaze away from his blood-soaked body and focus

back on Catalina. "You know my uncle was the Decapitator. It's in my blood."

She gives me a long study. "So why the tears just now? You don't seem like a crier."

"I know. I surprised myself." Sure I've gotten misty eyed, but the last time I actually cried big tears, my mom was in the hospital supposedly stabbed by the Decapitator. Just one of her many lies.

Catalina. My mother. Both experts at deceiving me. Something I will *never* allow to happen again. No one will ever control me like they have. Never again.

"I used to cry all the time," she tells me, then narrows her eyes. "Not anymore. I'm done being weak."

Catalina doesn't strike me as ever having been weak.

She turns away and strolls around the room, studying Dr. Issa and the rest of the area. "So now I have to figure out how to frame you for everything."

My left wrist slides free, and feverishly I begin working on my right as I keep her talking. "So why target the people you did?" She's already said as much, but it's all I can think of at the moment.

She curls her lip. "Prostitutes, homeless people, drug addicts. They're awful. I hate seeing them on the streets. I'm just trying to clean things up for everyone. Surely, you get that."

"I do," I go along.

She gives Dr. Issa's body another look. "I did *love* watching you stab that woman."

"That did feel good," I admit. At least afterward it did. "And you? Aren't you clever, following me, keeping me guessing, pretending to be my friend."

She breathes on her fingernails and cockily wipes them on her shirt.

"So who's next in your grand scheme?"

She turns to me, a little twinkle in her eye. "I've got some stuff on Tommy I'm going to threaten to take to the cops if he doesn't join forces with me."

My stomach muscles clench. "Tommy?"

"He's not so innocent. He's done a few things that he won't admit. But I know all about him. Actually, I'd love to beat the hell out of him first. Just to teach him a lesson."

She turns away to finger the items on the table. I yank my right wrist one last time, and the slickness from the blood allows it to slide free.

I keep my wrists behind my back as she turns around and then heads over to Dr. Issa. She slides the knife from his neck. "Now to frame you for all this and get out of here."

Quietly and quickly I get to my feet and snatch the bokken off the counter.

Catalina whirls around and narrows her eyes.

I lift the bokken, ready.

"Just because I don't have martial arts training doesn't mean I'm at a disadvantage. I did a little light aikido reading once I found out who you really were. 'One must respond to an attack and absorb it.' What kind of bullshit is that?"

If only she knew.

She wipes the blade on her cargo pants. "You. Will. Die."

We'll see about that.

I firm my grip on the bokken. *Breathe silently. Don't raise shoulders. Don't alert opponent.*

She pricks her skin with the blade—"Ooh, nice and sharp"—and charges me.

I move as one with her attack. Swerving back and to the left. Slashing the bokken down onto her wrists and propelling her forward.

She stumbles to catch her feet.

I control from the rear, bringing the bokken around, and slapping her in the ribs.

She inhales a sharp breath.

Good. Hopefully, I've broken one. Or maybe two.

Snarling, Catalina turns on me. She lunges, sweeping the large knife sideways through the air.

I block it with a downward cut. Recede. And maintain my focus on her.

She repositions the knife in front of her. Her grip tightening. Staring at me. Studying me.

I look into her eyes. Reading their disturbed depths.

She lurches to the left. Then quickly back to the right.

I drop to the ground. Roll. And sweep her ankles with the bokken.

Catalina falls hard on her ass. I rear back and pop her in the mouth.

She groans. Kicks. And her heel lands solidly against my shin. *Shit!* I grit my teeth as I bring the bokken up and crack her in the forearm right against the radial bone.

Catalina yelps and releases the knife.

I kick it. She scrambles for it. Grabs it. And turns to look at me.

I take a step back. Gauging her.

Craziness flashes through her eyes, and she licks the blood off her lip. "It is apparent to me that you're not going to die."

I loosen the grip on my bokken, rotate my wrist, and re-firm. "You are correct."

She yells and charges me.

I toss my bokken into my left hand, sweep-block her knife from the outside, and strike her in the voice box with the blade of my right hand.

She gags but maintains a death grip on her knife.

I grab her head, bend it downward and under, and throw her.

Catalina grunts, and all the air in her body rushes out as she lands on the knife.

I go completely still.

Slowly, she rolls to her back and sucks in a long, raspy breath. "Help me. . . ."

I don't move. I'm not going to help her. I want her to die. She's hurt too many people. She killed Dr. Issa. She deserves this.

Not taking her eyes off me, she grabs the handle of the knife, and with trembling hands tries to pull it out. Blood oozes and soaks her black T-shirt, and she gurgles. I remain where I am, listening to her raspy breaths and her gurgles, and watching the life slowly leave her as my heart seemingly beats in deep rhythm with it all.

It only takes a few minutes, and then she loses the battle with death and is gone.

Gradually her blood seeps out, spreading beneath her, widening until it almost touches Dr. Issa's blood.

I don't want their blood touching. But there's nothing I can do about it.

I don't know how much time passes as I stare at their blood, but eventually I move, taking my first step, slipping the bokken into its strap along my back.

I look around the place. The Taser, the tranq gun, the zip ties, the knife, the bat. Everything is here to frame Catalina for it all. Masked Savior, copycat, everything I've ever done, everything she's done. The cops find all this and they'll close the case.

I'll be free.

But what about Dr. Issa? How will his presence here be explained? I don't want his name tarnished. But I have no clue what to do.

I haven't touched anything but my bokken, so my fingerprints are nowhere. My ski mask is rolled on top of my head, so my hair is secure. No fibers anywhere. The chair, the zip ties she secured me with, the blood from my wrists—that's the only evidence I've been here.

I pick the chair up and lug it to the back door. I'll take it with me and dispose of it somewhere away from here.

At the back door I stop and give the room one last glance, and my gaze falls on Dr. Issa. I want to go over to him, look at him, and say good-bye, but I know I shouldn't. I can't risk any more evidence.

"Bye, Michael," I whisper. "I'll miss you."

Epilogue

THE WHOLE THING IS INVESTIGATED, AND A version of the truth comes out. Dr. Issa is thought to be the real Masked Savior and Catalina the copycat.

The task force concludes that Dr. Issa confronted her, they fought, and Catalina killed Dr. Issa and accidentally fell on the knife.

For the most part it's true. Dr. Issa is thought to be responsible for all the good acts done, and Catalina the vile bludgeonings.

One week later is Dr. Issa's memorial service. They cremate him and put his ashes in an urn. I don't hear a single thing said during the service, as focused on the urn as I am. It is truly incomprehensible that Dr. Issa's wonderful, handsome, intelligent self is now in that vase.

Victor and Daisy come with me to the service. Victor stands off to the side talking with a person he knows, and Daisy stands beside me.

"Do you ever just feel off?" my sister whispers.

"All the time," I tell her.

"What do you do about it?"

"Focus on what's right and good and normal."

She nods as if she's really digesting my response, and I ask, "Anything you want to talk about?"

She shakes her head—"Not now"—and wanders off to be with Victor.

My sister is definitely hiding something. I'll do exactly what I said. I'll be here, I'll be supportive, and I'll make sure she knows I *am* her ally.

Through the crowd I catch sight of Zach at the exact second he catches sight of me. At my mom's funeral I didn't want a bunch of hugs and attention, and so I give a small smile, just to let him know I'm thinking of him.

He takes that as his cue to walk to me, but I have no clue what to say.

Up close his eyes are red and swollen. "Thank you for coming," he whispers.

"Sure."

He swallows. His lip quivers. To hell with the no-hug thing. I step up and wrap my arms tightly around him, willing his agony into me. I'll take it. Gladly.

"This place," he mumbles into my hair, "it's a cancer to my family."

I nod. I know. I really know.

He pulls back and searches my eyes. I let him see every ounce of pain I feel for him. I don't hold anything back.

"We're moving," he murmurs.

Somehow the news doesn't surprise me.

He kisses me on the cheek. "See you around, Lane."

My heart clenches into one tight, sad muscle. "Yep, see ya."

Later when we all get home, Tommy is sitting in front of our house on his bike.

He's not so innocent. He's done a few things that he won't admit. But I know all about him.

Catalina's words come back and I shove them away. She did nothing but lie and play with me. That comment's just another manipulation. Plus, I'm not innocent. I've done things I won't admit.

"Want to get out of here?" he asks. "I'm thinking you and me need to bungee."

I nod, climb on his bike, and let him take me away.

Acknowledgments

Jenny Bent and Gemma Cooper: You two are a dream come true for this author. THANK YOU for being such great supportive agents. I am incredibly lucky to be working with you.

Patrick Price: I love you! You and I are two peas.

Melissa Jolly: You. Are. Wonderful! You seriously need to write a book titled *How to Be Excellent at Everything*.

Dana Kaye: You should coauthor that book with Melissa. :)

Marji Arzie: Even though I named my villain after you, you know I mean it with all the love in my heart. Thanks for being a great plotting partner.

Mara Anastas, Paul Crichton, Nicole Ellul, Michelle Fadlalla Leo, Jessica Handelman, Katherine Devendorf, Michael Rosamilia,

Sara Berko, Veda Kumarjiguda, Carolyn Swerdloff, Teresa Ronquillo: my amazing publishing team. Every one of you seriously rocks.

Young Adult Series Insiders (YASI): The thing about writers is that we are such a supportive community. I'm incredibly blessed to be surrounded by my fellow YASI sisters Jennifer Armentrout, Nina Berry, Anne Blankman, Martina Boone, Tracy Clark, Bree Despain, Kimberley Griffiths Little, and Claudia Gray.

My online friends/readers/followers: You make me smile every single day. I adore you!